She Fell in love With a

Dope Boy 2

Miss Candice

Previously

The sound of the stairs creaking told me that he was climbing them. As much as I tried to keep my focus on the gay dude doing makeup on my phone, I couldn't ignore the intoxicating scent that invaded my nostrils. Nor could I ignore the rapid beating of my heart.

"You ready?" I heard him say.

I kept my eyes on my phone, as I felt anger arising. Was Ashlee already fucking with him? I didn't know who's dick she was around here fucking and sucking. But I think I would have known if it Cass's dick was one of them. She couldn't be...not with the way she's been acting.

Ashlee perked up, "Yeah, where we goin? Shit it don't even matter—"

"Not you. Her," he said before snatching my phone from me and boldly stuffing it into the pocket of his designer shorts. "I told you, that phone shit gone be a serious problem in our relationship, sweetheart."

I looked up at him, ready to cuss him out. But the words got caught in my throat, and I was rendered speechless. His dreads were freshly retwisted. Cass stood over me with the stance of a God. The crisp white shirt he wore shined brightly against his deep, dark skin. He was so damn fine that I couldn't talk. Got damn. He owned a certain kind of sexy that could only be appreciated up close.

There was a slight furrow in his thick eyebrows when he repeated himself, "You ready?"

"Dawg, give me my phone," I said with a shaky voice.

Omni looked at me with concern written on her face, "Ryann...you okay?"

My hands grew clammy and I rolled my eyes before rubbing them on my black, skin tight, distressed jeans, "Yeah."

"You forgot about our date," he asked with a smile.

"What date?" I snapped. "Give me my phone."

"You want your phone? Come get it," he said before boldly jogging down the steps with my phone in his pocket.

I swallowed hard and sat there in a daze. In my photo gallery sat a few of my favorite pictures of him. You know, the ones I took without that nigga knowing? What if he went through my shit and saw them? What type of crazy, insane type bitch would I look like?

"Ryann...what the fuck...Ry," said Omni waving her hands in my face.

"Bitch that nigga is check-king for you! Ain't even look at my fine ass," said Ashlee.

I smacked Omni's small hands away and pushed myself up from my seat. I walked away from her and Ashlee while they asked me questions. I had to get my phone back. If I didn't, I'd fa sho look like a nut job.

He cockily looked over his shoulder at me while I jogged down the stairs. Knowing that I was following him, he got into his car anyway. I looked both ways down the street with my hands in the back pockets of my pants as I crossed, hoping Tiny wasn't lurking to snitch on me.

I knocked on the window of his car and the passenger door swung open. An invitation for me to get inside. I pulled my lips into my mouth and looked over my shoulder at Omni and Ashlee, watching my every move with scowls of confusion on their faces.

Omni held her hands up as to ask what was up and I just shrugged before heading over to the other side of the car.

I could tell that he was the type of nigga who didn't take no for an answer. He wanted me and he wouldn't have it any other way.

I climbed inside of the car and closed the door.

"Seat belt, sweetheart," he said as he cranked his engine up.

I could barely control myself in his presence. It annoyed the hell out of me too. I didn't know if I wanted to curse him out or ride his dick. Just like that, my focus had switched to sex.

I wondered if his dick was as dark as he was? I wondered if it had a curve to it? Or if it was thick and veiny? Did the vein wrap around the shaft? Or was it one thick vein, running from the base of his dick, down to his balls? I wondered if he had a perfect mushroom head? Or if the surgeon who'd done his circumcision wasn't precise enough with his scalpel? But was he even circumcised to begin with?

"You need help with that seat belt?" he asked, snapping me out of my nasty thoughts.

"What? I'm not riding anywhere with you. I'm just here for my phone."

"I told you last night we would talk today. Why are you actin' brand new again shorty? Shit, last night I had you hyperventilating and shit. Now you acting like you want me to get away from you. Ya distraction get in your head or what?"

"I don't remember anything from last night," I said as I sat on my hands trying to control the sweating.

He rubbed his chin, "Yeah, you were drunk as fuck."

He then began to run everything down to me, word for word. A smile had spread wide across my face against my will. I didn't want him to see how open I was but hell, it was apparent that he had already seen that side of me.

"What you say about not riding with a nigga?" he asked as I realized we were now moving.

I was so wrapped up in my thoughts about his dick and everything else, that I didn't even realize that we were off the block. He stopped at a stop sign then leaned over and pulled my seatbelt on. I couldn't move. I was in a paralyzed state, frozen by the feel of the thick, curly hairs on his arm brushing against the bareness of collarbone. His scent crept up my nose once again, and I subconsciously deeply inhaled.

"Smell good, don't it?" he said with a smirk as he gripped the steering wheel, preparing to take off.

"What do you want?" I asked, trying to steer away from how weird I was acting.

"I think you already know the answer to that question, baby," he replied. "If you'd rather hear me speak it; I want you."

I sighed and looked out of the window, trying to find at least a piece of myself. Why couldn't I function as a regular person with this nigga? I was so nervous that I couldn't even look at him.

"Oh, I get it," he said after a few seconds of silence. "You're nervous. You don't fuck with dope boys. What? Riding shotty got you shook? Trust, sweetheart, you are in good hands with me. Niggas want me dead, but not enough to pull the trigger."

How did he know I didn't like dope boys? After he ran down everything that happened last night, I could tell that he had done his homework on me. He knew so much about me, yet I knew nothing about him with the exception to the address of his residence.

"No...that's not it," I managed to say. I pulled my lips into my mouth and shook my head from side to side then said, "I can't even fuckin' talk."

Cass reached over and pulled my hands from up under my thighs. As soon as his hand touched my palm, I pulled away.

"Your hands are drenched in sweat," he said with furrowed eyebrows. "If it's not that, then what? How much *do* you like me, Ms. Ryann?"

"Too much," I mumbled. "At this point...I'm not even sure if I could call it a crush."

"Infatuation? I tend to have that effect on pretty girls," he cockily said.

I nervously giggled."Baby, I'm infatuated with you too," he said, as he grabbed my hand again and intertwined his fingers with mine despite how sweaty it was. "Now, let me get to know you—"

Woop! Woop!

I looked in the rearview mirror and there was a police car riding behind us with the siren on.

"Fuck these niggas want?" said Cass as his hand slipped out of mine.

"We straight?" I asked, worried about drugs being in the car.

"Perfectly fine," he reassured me as he pulled over with his eyes narrowed in on the rearview. "Unless they try to fuck with me over the gun in my glovebox."

A gun? In the glovebox? How many bodies are on that mothafucka? I prayed like hell they didn't ask to search the car. I prayed from the moment they stepped out of their car, until they were asking us to step out of the vehicle.

Cass kept asking them what it was that they were pulling him over for, but they said nothing. He didn't want to get out, but I did. I didn't want to give them a hard time. They killed young black men for shit like that. If Cass was killed...right next to me... I don't think I'd ever be able to get a grip on my sanity again.

It took me almost a year to recover from the horror of finding my parents dead. If Cass was killed in front of me, by some scary ass cops, I would lose my mind.

My heart beat rapidly against my chest as he continued to argue with them about not stepping out of the car. When I moved my hand to grab hold of his, the cop next to my window drew his gun from the holster and pointed it at me. I immediately put my trembling hands up, scared out of my mind.

"Hands where we can see them," yelled the white cop.

"Yo, is that shit necessary?" yelled Cass as he put his hands up.

"Slowly step out of the vehicle," said the cop standing at Cass's window.

I couldn't move though. The gun in my face... it kept me planted. I sat there, petrified. Paralyzed with fear. I could hear Cass telling me it was alright and to step out of the car. His voice calmed me, while the cop with his gun in my face, who was steady yelling at me, did nothing to help the situation. I couldn't move. Not with that gun in my face. Not faced with the same fate my parents were faced with. One bullet to the right side of their heads was what ended them. Ironic how this police officer stood on the right side of me, with a gun pointed at my head.

"Get that gun out of her face, fuck nigga. You're scaring her," said Cass through clenched teeth. "Ryann, unbuckle your seat belt and get out, sweetheart. I got you. I told you, with me you are safe. This nigga ain't gone pop shit. I promise on my fuckin' life."

The certainty in his voice was astounding. How could he say that? How could he be so sure? But I believed him, although the cop could do whatever he damn well pleased.

I took a deep breath and unbuckled my seat belt.

"That's it baby. Block the pussy and his gun out, aight? We straight. We good," said Cass as he too slowly got out of the car.

Finally, my feet were planted on the ground. As soon as they hit the pavement though, the cop put his gun away and shoved me into the car.

Cass yelled, "Get yo fuckin' hands off of her, my nigga—"

As soon as he said something, the other cop threw him onto the hood of the car, "Stay your black ass right here, or I swear to God Detroit will have one less bad guy."

I watched him pull Cass's arms behind his back and handcuff him. Yet, they hadn't even told us why they were pulling us over.

The cop walked away and began to check the car. I swallowed a heavy lump in my throat, trying to block out the cop's grabby hands. They were all over me. Violated. He had violated the fuck out of me.

"That's enough," said Cass, tightlipped, looking over at us. The cop finally stepped back and told me to stand up straight.

He asked for my name and I gave it to him.

"As in relation to Chance 'Goose' Mosley?" he asked with sarcasm.

"Yes," I said with an eye roll.

"Oh, we've hit big, Ben," he yelled to his partner.

"Damn right we hit good, partner. I've found me a gun," said the cop on the inside of the car. "I'm sure there are a few bodies on this bad baby—

"It's mine," I blurted out, not thinking about what I was saying.

I was out of my mind at this point. I couldn't be thinking straight. Cass shot me a look as to say 'What the fuck are you doing?' I slightly shrugged, and before I knew it, I was being thrown back up against the car.

"Yo, what the fuck I say about the way you handlin' her, G? The burner is mine," Cass yelled.

"Oh no it's not. Ben, we've got us a Mosley here. They are notorious for gun charges. It's hers. Ain't that right, sugar?" said the cop as he put handcuffs on me.

I didn't realize how fucked I was until I was being tossed in the back of the squad car. I had taken a gun charge for a nigga I barely even knew. What is wrong with me?

- Ryann -

"What happened to your face?" asked Cass, standing outside of the police station, with a frown on his face.

I looked a complete mess. I had to stay in a nasty ass jail cell overnight. I didn't get any sleep and I cried the whole time I was there. I didn't like the headspace jail put me in. I was miserable and above all, terrified.

I gripped my closed fist around my belongings bag and looked away, "Boyfriend said I fell... I'm guessing after I got out of the car with you."

I hated that he was seeing me like this. I was too embarrassed and felt downright ugly and nasty. In addition to my scars being exposed, my hair was all over my head and I'm sure I had bags under my eyes. I knew my lips were probably cracked and dry and I was on straight bum shit. The black distressed jeans I had on were dingy and the fitted gray tank I had on was dirty too.

"Fell huh?" he asked, rubbing at the stubble on his chin. "Oh, aight."

He approached me with slightly opened arms and then wrapped them around me. I felt such a sense of security in his arms. I didn't know if it was because jail had been straight hell or what, but, I was happy to be there. Happy he had gotten me out of there when he did.

"Thank you," I said with my voice slightly muffled by his black t-shirt.

"Nothing to thank me for, sweetheart," he said as he pulled away and intertwined his fingers with mine.

From the outside looking in, you would think we knew each other or something. The way he responded to me was like how someone would respond to their girlfriend. He was holding my hand for crying out loud. He was such a damn gentleman and a thug wrapped all into one.

I should have pulled away, but I didn't. I happily interlocked my fingers with his. I didn't know what I was doing or why I was doing it, but I went along with it. I knew I was in the wrong, considering I'm still with Dinero. Speaking of him, he's probably going crazy trying to find me. I wondered if anyone knew what was going on.

"Do my people know?" I asked Cass.

"Yeah, they know. I linked with them niggas as soon as y'all pulled away," said Cass as we walked towards his Benz. "We had a sit down. Them niggas ain't happy." He glanced at me as he opened the passenger door, "Neither am I."

I wasn't too happy with myself. I don't know what in the hell possessed me to do what I did. But listen, if Cass would have taken ownership over that gun, he'd still be in there. If it wasn't for the gun being clean and it being my first offense, they would have kept me longer. They had a real hard-on for me. The moment they found out I was a Mosley, it was game time. None of the cops in the police station were fond of me and I lost count of how many of them tried to get me to say that the gun belonged to either Cass...or get this...even Goose.

Goose had so many gun charges against him, that they were dying to plant another one on him to have a reason to lock him up for the rest of his life. They hated him and everyone related to him. They didn't give a fuck about me being cute or none of that. They dogged me out, gave me the nastiest mattress and the thinnest blanket in that bitch.

They treated me like a criminal. Had it not been for Cass sending his lawyer up there to get me out, I would still be there. The gun was clean, but they were purposely holding me, telling me that there were some technicalities they were sorting through. All lies. As soon as the lawyer came to represent me, they let me out not even ten minutes later. I practically ran out of that place. I never wanted to be in a predicament like that again.

"You jumped the gun," said Cass as I slid into the car. "But we gone work on that."

He closed the door and I fastened my seatbelt.

I knew them niggas were talking all kinds of shit. They taught me better than this. My brothers taught me to never make anyone else's shit my shit. They didn't even want me involved in what they had going on. There were only a select few who really knew I was a Mosley. If you weren't from east seven mile, then you didn't even know I existed. That is why the cop was so surprised when I told him I was related to Goose.

My brothers kept me on hush-hush simply because they wanted me safe. They protected me with everything in them, yet here I was putting myself in shit. Getting myself involved in someone else's mess. Someone I didn't even know.

Thing is, I didn't have to know Cass to know that I didn't want him locked up. I'd take another petty charge if that meant keeping him out of prison, or out of a grave. In most cases, niggas like Cass... they never make it to the jail cell. A cop would murder him before they locked him up.

Seconds later, Cass was climbing into his driver seat. He reached into the backseat and grabbed a bottle of water.

Handing it to me he asked, "You take gun charges for all the cats you talk to?"

I cracked the bottle open and took a few sips before replying, "I don't take charges for anybody."

"What changed?" he asked as he backed out of the parking space.

I met you. I wanted to say it, but I wouldn't dare.

Shrugging, I decided I didn't want to have a voice. Instead, I chugged the entire bottle of water, then asked for another.

"Never do anything like that again, Ryann," he said in a demanding tone.

He was upset. Why? I'd gotten him out of a bind. I expected him to thank me. I thought he would appreciate me looking out for him, but it was apparent that he didn't appreciate it at all. Anger rose from the pit of my soul as I began to feel my eyes sting with tears.

Did this cocky, black, nappy headed son of a bitch not know what I went through? The humiliation. The horrible conditions I was forced to live in for twelve hours? I was sleep deprived. I starved myself. I dealt with disrespect. And above all of that, I could possibly be single now. I risked losing Dinero for him. I risked losing my freedom for him. I took ownership of a gun I knew nothing about. It could have had a dozen bodies on it. Knowing this, I took the charge anyway.

And for him.

For someone who sat next to me, gripping the steering wheel with a frown on his face.

"You're welcome," I snapped with a slight chuckle.

"I don't praise stupidity," he replied with a voice as cold as ice.

"Stupidity," I said with my face screwed up.

He glanced at me, "I just committed a crime with that same gun a couple days ago, shorty. Shot a nigga straight through the back of his hand. Before I made the rational decision to spare his life, I was getting ready to blow his top off."

A cool chill ran down my spine as reality really set in. It could have all been over. In a matter of minutes, life as I've known it could have been over. I swallowed a knot in my throat and again asked for another water. He jerked his head towards the back of the car, telling me to grab it.

Cass stopped at a red light and reached in the middle compartment of his car. He pulled my phone from it and handed it to me.

"Boyfriend is relentless," he said.

I looked back at him with raised eyebrows, wondering if he had answered. Questioning if he'd answered it without actually asking him.

"I let that bitch ring until the battery died."

I let out a breath of relief and stuffed the phone into the back pocket of my dusty black jeans.

"Time is of the essence. How much of it do you plan on wasting?" he sternly asked me as he stared at the side of my face.

I didn't have words for that neither, so I simply shrugged.

Cass thick tongue brushed up against his full bottom lip and he asked, "You want to eat?"

"I want to shower," I replied as I began to fumble with the top of the water bottle.

He placed his hand on top of mine and said, "Always so nervous."

The placement of his hand didn't calm my nerves. If anything, it made them go even crazier. I could hear the sound of my heart beating through my ears. The beat of my heart was the only thing I could hear. While his hand rested on top of mine, time moved like molasses, yet the beat of my heart thumped at a million beats per second. It was as if through his touch, I could feel every nerve ending in his body. His hand on top of mine... it made my vagina jump in ways only sexual touching made it jump in.

Then he pulled his hand away and I could breathe again. Time moved at its normal pace.

I sucked in a gust of air and placed a piece of hair behind my ear. I could feel Cass's eyes on me, but I refused to look his way. I knew that I would get lost in those black irises of his.

"You aight?" he asked.

I nodded and continued to fumble with the bottle cap.

The rest of the ride to my house was quiet. From the corner of my eye, I could see Cass steal glances at me every two minutes. By the look on his face, he had questions. He wanted to talk, but my body language was uninviting. I sat there unmoving with my eyes on the road. Often times, I had to remind myself to breath.

I wondered if I would ever be able to be myself around him. I wondered if this phase would change. This... this infatuation. The paralytic state it put me in.

As soon as Cass's Benz turned onto the block, all eyes fell on us. My identity stayed hidden behind the dark tints, but not for long. I would be exposed the moment my feet hit the pavement. I would be on the receiving end of questioning gazes and a set of fiery eyes which belonged to Dinero, who sat on my porch with my family.

The car came to a halt in front of the house and I didn't move an inch. My brothers stood to their feet and began to tread down the stairs with Dinero following behind them.

"How do I...How can I reach you? I asked, stammering over my words as the four men with frowns on their faces got closer and closer to the car.

"313-555-7109," he replied.

I repeated the number in my head as I grabbed hold of the door handle. Before I could get out, Cass touched my shoulder, "Call me tonight."

I nodded and got out of the car.

Juice sent Cass a head nod as I walked right by them, ignoring the judgmental looks on their faces. I avoided eye contact with Dinero, but he was on my heels. I wouldn't be able to avoid him for too long. What I did decide to do was keep it all the way real with him. Shit, Cass took my phone and I went to get it. That is what happened, right? What he will give a fuck more about is the fact that I took a gun charge for him. I planned on keeping it real about that as well. I knew that whatever the consequence might have been they would be lighter on my end. That is why I did it.

"Fuck everything we talked about, huh?" asked Juice as they followed me into the house.

I sighed, and rolled my eyes, "Let me shower before y'all try to school me, aight? Besides, I'm a grown ass woman, I do what I want—"

"Even in a relationship?" asked Dinero with a scowl on his face. "What about us, Ry?"

What about us? That is what I wanted to ask. This thing with Dinero, didn't even feel like a relationship. We'd been cool for days and he has yet to touch me. No sex and barely any affection. Maybe it was because I had been so cold to him, but shit, whatever the case we should have more going on than we did.

"Shower. All I want is a shower," I said, as I continued to ignore every one of them.

*

I plugged my phone into the charger before easing my body into the scalding hot bubble bath. Resting my back against the back of the tub, I closed my eyes and let the heat massage my tensed muscles. First, I wanted to soak and then I would let hot water beat against my skin. To be honest, I was really trying to prolong things because I did not want to face Dinero. My brothers, I could deal with. Facing Dinero would be like hopping onto an emotional rollercoaster. I could talk all of that tough shit, but I dreaded the look of sadness in his eyes that awaited me. He wanted this to work so bad, but yet, I kept pulling away.

I couldn't be the woman he wanted me to be. It's not like I haven't been telling him that. I told him days ago that I wasn't in love with him and he thought I was masking my true feelings. I was keeping it real with him. He's one of those men who thought he could make a woman fall in love with him. He showers me with compliments and gifts, thinking that materialistic shit moved me. But that's not the way it works. It's either there, or it's not. And I wasn't there with Dinero. I didn't think I ever would be. Not with someone as captivating as Cass in my life.

Knock. Knock. Knock.

Before I could respond to the knocking, the bathroom door was being pushed open. Dinero walked inside with his shoulders slumped over and a blank expression on his face. But there was so much sadness swimming in his eyes that the shit ate me up.

He sat on side of the tub and grabbed my loofa. He lathered it up with Dove body wash and began to run it over my shoulder blades. I wanted to protest, but I couldn't deny how good it felt. It could be that I hadn't been touched this way in weeks.

"What do I have to do, Ryann?" asked Dinero. "If you want me to clean the apartment up, I will. If you want me to spend more time or to invest more into your dreams, I will. What is it?"

I opened my eyes and sighed, "Dinero—"

"We were good, shorty. Before that shit with Tiny, I had you. You were here, now I don't know where the fuck you are," he said cutting me off. "I care about you way too much to sit back and just let this shit happen to us."

Why did he want to force it? Forcing love didn't make things better. If anything, forcing it would push me even further away than I already was.

He carried on, "You got me out here lookin' like a true ass sucka, Ry. Why? Because you don't trust me anymore—

I cut him off, "Not on purpose, D. Let me explain, aight?! I owe you an explanation. I'll give you that. Cass took my phone and I followed him for it. Before I knew it, we were off the block and being pulled over by the police. They found a gun and I took ownership over it. Why? Because I don't have any offenses. I would get a slap on the wrist, whereas...I don't know what would have happened to him. Not that I should care," I shook my head. "It was stupid. I know that. But that's all that happened, Dinero. I didn't purposely go back on my promise to you."

"That shit is over and done with now, Ry," said Dinero with furrowed eyebrows. "Ain't it?"

I nodded, "Nothing happened. Relax."

He tried to keep the bitching up, but I cut that shit short and told him that I just wanted to enjoy my shower. When he said we could just continue the conversation after, I told him to dead it. I didn't want to dwell on bullshit. I had been pretty much over the conversation since before it started. Dinero nodded and walked out of the bathroom, sulking. Ugh.

*

Thirty minutes and a shower later, I was dressed in pajama shorts and tank. I thought I was about to curl up in my bed to get some sleep, but my brothers had another thing in mind for me. Dinero was even gone. I'm sure they put his ass out.

"I'm legit tired as fuck. Please, I do not want to do—

"Sit down," barked Goose, startling me.

You think I kept talking shit? Oh baby, no. I sucked my teeth and sat my mad ass right on the sofa across from all of my brothers. I sat there with my elbows pressed against my knees, annoyed.

Goose moved his head from side to side, cracking his neck. He then moved his shoulders and cracked his knuckles. Juice sat back on the couch with his arm stretched out over the back of it, with flaring nostrils. Adrien sat pinching the bridge of his nose, biting down on his teeth, making his jaw muscles flex. They were pissed. So much was being said without being verbalized. I had disappointed them.

"You aight, lil sis?" asked Goose with a little smirk on his face.

"I'm tired—

"Nah," he began to roughly poke himself in his temple. "I'm talkin' about upstairs and shit."

I sighed, "I fucked up. I get it."

"Naw, sis, you can't get it," said Juice finally speaking up.

Goose began to pace the living room floor, mumbling under his breath. It was kind of hard to pay attention to what Adrien had begun to say. Goose is impulsive as hell. He would never put hands on me, but he'd throw some shit across the room in a heartbeat.

"I saw you watching the nigga all googly eyed and shit at the party," said Goose cutting Juice off. "I just took it as a lil' petty ass crush. But you out here doin dumb shit."

"Do you even know that nigga?" asked Adrien. "Thank God the banger wasn't dirty. They would have thrown you under the jail off the strength of you being a Mosley in general."

"In relation to Chance Goose Mosley," animatedly mumbled Goose, repeating what the cop had said to me, before yelling, "Fuck they meanin..."

"Calm down, G," said Juice standing up.

I didn't mean to upset Goose like this. I didn't even know how he knew they mentioned him. Maybe Cass told him. I would have never told him they said something about him. I hadn't told them anything about what went on during my arrest besides the fact that I had taken the gun charge for Cass. I wasn't going to share anything with them, either. Especially not the part about the cop's grabby hands. They would shoot the whole damn police station up.

I handled all of my brothers based on their personalities. And Goose? Goose was the most fragile of the three. Anything would make him snap.

I jumped up from the couch and approached him. I grabbed him by his shirt and pulled him into a hug. He was reluctant for a few seconds. But then I began to shush him and tell him that I was sorry and wouldn't do it again.

*

After convincing my brothers that I would never do anything like that again, they went on about their business. Although it was early in the day, I closed the drapes, turned the central air up high, went into my room, crawled up under a blanket, and tried to fall asleep.

As tired as I was, I couldn't sleep. My mind wouldn't let me as I kept repeating Cass's number over and over in my head so that I wouldn't forget it. Saving it to my phone would have been easier, but for the sake of avoiding more drama in my failing relationship, I decided that simply memorizing it would be better.

Anyway, Cass had consumed my every damn thought. Every time I closed my eyes, I saw him standing in front of the police station waiting for me. I thought about the way his hand felt sitting on top of mine and I thought about the way the word sweetheart sounded slipping off those full lips of his.

I needed to call my man, but I wanted to call Cass. He said to call him tonight, but I couldn't wait. I was about to be on some straight up thirsty bitch shit, but I did not care. He said time was of the essence right? But then again, I did feel like calling him would be a bit much, so instead, I just shot him a quick text so that he would have my phone number.

Me (1:47PM): Hey, this is Ryann just texting so that you'll have my number.

Not even a full minute had passed before my phone began to ring. A smile spread wide across my face as I stared at the number I'd been memorizing on my screen.

I shifted around in my bed to get comfortable before I answered, "Hello?"

"Come outside," he demanded.

"Cass—

"A nigga ain't trying to hear anything but, *aight Cass here I come,*" he said cutting me off.

I chewed on my bottom lip and shook my head. I needed to stay my ass away from him, at least during the day. Shit the block was slapping and Dinero had a personal snitch. I didn't want to deal with anymore drama so I told Cass I couldn't come out.

"I'm tired, I didn't get any sleep. I was just texting so you could lock me in," I said.

"Get your rest, sweetheart. Later, I'm not taking no for an answer."

Later I'd probably be tied up with Dinero's ass. I wanted nothing more than to be with Cass, trust me. I was finally getting everything I wanted. His attention. His conversation. Something was happening. A friendship? Possible a relationship? A bitch was jumping the gun, fa sho.

I giggled a little, "Okay, Cass."

*

I was chilling on the porch with Dinero when this bitch Tiny and her flock of hood rats began to walk up the block all loud and obnoxious. I was dumb annoyed. Maybe it was because of who they were talking to.

"Heeeey Cass, you look nice tonight. You want to go downtown?" said one of them.

I looked across the street and Cass was leaning on his beamer looking down at his phone. When my phones notification ringer went off, I just knew it was him texting about how we were supposed to link tonight.

"Don't he though? Fine as fuck," said Tiny.

Dinero snorted and I frowned, "What?"

"Fucking hood rats, man," he said before draping arm over my shoulder. "You want to go in the crib?" He licked his lips and looked down my tank, "A niggas been wanting to slide in for a while now."

I heard everything Dinero was saying, but my attention was on the shit going on across the street.

"You heard me?" asked Dinero.

"In a bit. I'm enjoying this fresh air."

Cass had barely said five words to them bitches, but they were now leaning up on his car flirting with him. My phone buzzed again, and Dinero snatched it off the small Bristol table.

"What time is it," he said as he unlocked my screen. "Who is 555-7190?"

I grabbed the phone from Dinero, hoping Cass hadn't made it known that it was him. I let out a sigh of relief when I saw that he hadn't said anything that would give us away.

(313)555-7190 (9:12PM): Get rid of 'em.

(313)555-7190 (9:13PM): Before I get rid of 'em myself.

I swallowed and shook my head, "I don't know. They must have the wrong number." I paused, "It's almost 9:15. Why? You got somewhere to go?"

I had been trying to get rid of Dinero all damn night, but he was stuck to me like glue. I knew that any chances of kicking it with Cass was deaded as soon as Dinero picked me up, carried me into the house, and told me that here was the only place he needed to be.

- Cass -

"He didn't hit her; she was drunk as hell and fell on her face," said Luck, on the other end of my phone.

I wiped sleep from my eyes and sat up, "Good looks my nigga."

After dropping Ryann off at the crib, I had Luck look into the surveillance over at Club 211 to make sure what Ryann's pussy ass boyfriend said was legit. Had he called with some other news, I would have slid down on the nigga and did him dirty. But since the story checked out, I was satisfied.

"Fa sho. When we linking, G?"

"I'll hit your line in about three or four hours. I got some shit to handle," I told him before we ended our phone call.

I sat up against the headboard as I went through my phone, expecting a text from ol' girl, but I got nothing. I snorted and shook my head. Last night, we were supposed to link, but since she was wrapped up with her weak ass nigga, I decided to stick dick to one of the bitches in the hood. I didn't want to, but I needed something to distract me from spazzing.

It was just after ten o'clock in the morning. I had a meeting in about two hours I had to get to so I texted a few niggas back and got out of bed. I slid my feet into my Gucci slides, and headed over to the window to pull the drapes back. As soon as I did, I flinched at the sight of Jane's slut ass smiling wide, waving.

Bitch was a crazy one, on God. Ever since I let her suck my dick, she's been on another level. This was my fourth time opening my drapes to her waving at me like she'd been standing there waiting for me to open up. I didn't even wave back at the bitch, I frowned and walked off. I should have known better than to let her slob me up. A red flag was raised when she basically asked me to piss in her mouth. But shit, I just thought she was one of those weird ass freaky white bitches. I didn't know she would end up on some stalk shit.

On top of her waving at me every morning damn near, she'd been leaving me notes in my mailbox. Freaky shit about how she couldn't wait to feel my fat dick in her ass and how she couldn't wait to swallow my kids again. My man's Billy had no idea how much of a slut his wife was. I low key felt kinda bad for buddy.

*

"I'll take it," I said to realtor sitting across from me with a judgmental smirk on her face.

Scotty, my lawyer, leaned over and whispered in my ear, "It's ten thousand over budget, Mr. Banks."

I shifted in my seat, adjusting my slacks, "Don't tell me how to spend my money, Scotty. You're overpaid, yet you haven't pointed that out to me."

The building was indeed overpriced, considering the work needed to be done on it, but I wanted it. As soon as I walked into the property, I felt like it was perfect. I'd gone through five buildings and not one of them gave me the feeling this one did. Granted, it needed a little work done to it, but it was the one.

Georgetta, the realtor, adjusted her bifocal glasses and cleared her throat, "There is an extensive credit check that must be done, with a thirty dollar credit check fee. If your credit is under seven fifty, you will not qualify."

I chuckled, "Run it, darling. I'm overqualified."

I was about ten seconds away from snapping on her. She had been gawking at me with judgmental eyes since I walked in the building. She didn't care that I had on a designer suit and was stomping with one of the most prestige lawyers in the state of Michigan. All she could see was a thug with money.

I didn't have a high school diploma, but that didn't mean I was a stupid nigga. I was a young black man, but that didn't mean I had fucked up credit. When people looked at me all they saw was my black skin, thick dreads, ink and bulging muscles. They couldn't see what was underneath the exterior. That shit annoyed the fuck out of me when I was trying to cordially make business decisions.

"Are you sure? Checking it would only—

"Yo, you serious right now? I said run it," I said before shifting in my seat again. A niggas dick was dead ass uncomfortable in these slacks. "My money ain't good enough for you, huh? Yo, Scot, call corporate on this bird. Let 'eem know we're about to hit 'em off with a discrimination suit."

Her eyes widened in surprise, "I wasn't discriminating against you, Mr. Banks. I just—

I interrupted her, "The only thing you need to be doing is processing my application, darling."

"Keep it cool, man," whispered Scotty.

"Fuck all lat," I shot back with a frown on my face. "A nigga trying to do something positive out here, and mafuckas just can't respect it."

Georgetta knew what I wanted the property for. The whole time I walked around the building, I talked to Scotty about my vision. She didn't seem interested and probably thought I only wanted to open it up to clean up some money. If I wanted this to be a boutique, a beauty salon, or some shit like that, then definitely. But not with this Boys and Girls home.

That's what I was doing—trying to open up a group home for neglected children. I wanted this bitch to be top of the line, employing only the best of the best. I wanted outstanding caregivers with top notch credentials. I wanted on-site healthcare and all that. I never wanted a kid to feel the way I felt growing up, like I wasn't shit. I was mistreated and abused and by mafuckas who was supposed to take care of me.

This group home was going to be so official that the kids staying in it wouldn't be so wrapped up in wanting to be adopted. I wanted to offer kids the opportunities I wasn't offered. I wanted to set 'em up with scholarships and all that. I wasn't going to stop with this one facility neither; I wanted them all over the fuckin' country.

"How long does the credit check take, Ms. Whittaker?" asked Scotty.

"We will be in touch within forty-eight hours," she replied with her eyes on the iPad in her hands, rather than on me.

"Aight, we up, Scotty baby," I said as I pushed myself up from the chair I sat in. "Ay, Georgetta, in case you've caught a case of amnesia or in case you might be colorblind or some shit," I paused and leaned across the desk she sat at. "You are African American, darlin. We come from the same struggles, I'm just trying to rise above it."

As expected, she didn't even look up at me. I could tell that she was nervous by the shaking of her finger as she swiped around on her iPad. Her bottom lip quivered and through her glasses, I could see her eyes get misty.

*

As soon as I pulled up on the block, the first person I spotted amongst the forty plus posted up was Ryann. Maybe she stood out to me because she was sitting on her porch with her fuck ass nigga. She had the nerve to be straddling the nigga like I wasn't liable to pull up at any given moment. Same shit she was on last night. It had me wondering—was she serious with this bozo now?

I parked behind Luck's whip and hopped out. All these mafuckas were posted up, yet my attention stayed on her. Her attention was on me as well, but when dawg looked past her to see what it was she was looking at, she quickly wrapped her arms around his neck on some caking shit. I smirked and nodded at Juice who sat on the porch with his shorty too.

He yelled, "What it is, bruh? Come rap with me before you leave the hood, aight?"

"Fa sho," I yelled back before slapping hands with Luck.

"What's good, G?" he asked before taking a pull of his blunt. "Fuck were you on earlier? I hit ya line like ten times."

"Business," I said as I took the blunt he was passing me from him. "What it is G? You blowin up my hitter like you my old lady or some shit," I said with a light chuckle.

"Get the fuck outta here, fool," he said with a smirk waving me off. "Shit, nigga I thought you were caught up or something."

"Nah, I was handlin' a lil B.I."

The only person that knew about the group home was Scotty and that's because he's my lawyer. I wasn't embarrassed by it or shit like that. I'm just the type of cat that don't go around running my lips about shit I got going on. When it's solid and off the ground, I'll rap about it. Until then, I'm keeping it to myself. A lot of mafuckas look at me and only see the savagery. Take that goofy Wavy for example. Soon as I told the nigga to drop five k off at the church, he came at me with that jokey shit, thinking it was a game. There is more to me than meets the eye.

Luck nodded across the street, "What that gun charge looking like?"

I sucked my teeth, "Ain't no gun charge. Shorty's cool. Shits crazy, uh? Had the shoe been on the other foot, I would still be in that bitch."

"Hell yeah, you already know what it is. We young wanted niggas," he said with a chuckle.

"Yoooo, you niggas heard about what happened to Mitch the Snitch," yelled Wavy skipping up the block like a fuckin' kid. "Nigga got a bad batch. Straight battery acid."

"Yo, ain't that was Maino and Rome who gave that nigga the shit?" said one of the foot soldiers, dribbling a ball.

"Oh fuck, you right dawg. I heard them niggas slid through trying to see if big homie knew it was them who stole that bag off Keys," said Wavy.

"Them niggas been seen in the hood and I'm just now hearing about it," said Luck with a mug on his face. "Yo, you hear this shit G?"

I shrugged, "I hear it. Don't really give a fuck about it though."

Maino and Rome would be dealt with. I didn't give a fuck enough to run around looking for the niggas. They were the type of idiots who would end up showing their faces in the hood sooner than later. Luck was standing there fuming about petty money like them dudes were a serious problem.

I was more bothered by them giving Mitch the Snitch a bad batch than I was about them snatching my ten K from Keys. Like I said, they would be dealt with. To get my blood boiling and all that would be a waste of time.

Luck yelled hysterically, "Bro, what you sayin—"

"What I'm saying is," I paused and pulled from the blunt. "Is that I don't give a fuck. Peep, if any of you niggas see one of them...Rome or Maino...or shit, both of 'eem... split their fuckin' wigs, aight?" I told them with my eyebrows raised. I slapped Luck on the shoulder, "Do me a favor and stop giving them bums so much attention, aight famo? We got more pressing issues to worry about."

"Nah, I'm just saying them niggas disrespected."

"They disrespected Keys. They knew off top that Keys would catch the consequences behind losing my money," I passed him the blunt. "Be easy."

I walked away, heading across the street. Ryann glanced over her shoulder at me coming and tensed up. Her soft ass nigga noticed and began to rub on her back. One of the bitches on the porch stood up, smoothing her hair over, and adjusting her coochie cutter shorts.

I stepped in front of the house and said, "Go grab Juice for me, sweetheart."

Ryann looked over her shoulder at me and asked, "You talking to me?"

"C'mon shorty... that is what I call you, right?" I asked with a smirk.

"Yo, my mans, you don't see me sitting here?" he said with added bass to his voice

I glanced away and then back at Ryann ignoring the nigga she sat on, "You gone go grab ya brother for me? Or do this nigga gotta fuckin' leash on you?"

I was popping off recklessly, I admit it. I was a little salty because she had her ass pressed all against the niggas crotch, the same fuckin' way she was last night. She was playing me, and I didn't like to be played.

Ryann sucked her teeth and got up, "A leash? Nigga who—

"Hey Cass, you want Juice? I'll go grab him for you. I don't have a leash or a nigga to worry about," said the girl in the short shorts with a wink before heading into the house.

"Good looks, darling. I appreciate it," I replied with a smile.

From the corner of my eye, I could see Ryann's nostril's flare.

"Bitch, you real funny," said Ryann.

Baby was stupid heated. But for the fuck what, right? Shit, will it take me sticking dick to her cousin for her to get her mind right? On the real though, I would never disrespect baby like that. I respected her far too much. In my eyes, Ryann was to be treated like fuckin' royalty. She was of a rare breed—a got damn thoroughbred. Too much of a thoroughbred to be fuckin' with a joker like the dude she was so bent on.

"Calm down, boo-baby. You know how she is," said her boyfriend, standing up and wrapping his arms around her. "This nigga just trying to be funny. Ay, dawg you being disrespectful—

I ran my tongue over the corner of my mouth, "Peep game, home boy... You really don't want to do this right now."

"I'm just sayin', my G. Respect is respect and right now you not only disrespecting my girl, you're disrespecting me," he said pointing to his buffed up chest, like a real ass goofy.

Ryann put her hands around his waist and told him to chill out. She was trying to save the fuck nigga, but to me, it looked like he didn't want saving.

"Disrespectful would be snatching you up and beatin ya face against one of these bricks," I calmly replied with my hands stuffed in the pockets of my shorts. "You ain't met disrespectful yet, pussy."

"What you just say to me—"

Ryann grabbed him by the arm and quickly pulled him down the stairs away from me.

"Just go to work, babe. Please, don't do this right now," I could hear Ryann say.

"Yeah, bum, listen to your shorty. Fuck around and lose yo life if you want to, G," I said with a slight chuckle. Turning away from them, I looked up on the porch at Juice's girl and nodded at her, "Wassup? You aight darlin'?"

She coyly nodded with her lips perched, "Mmhmm, I'm alright. Juice should be right out, he only went to the bathroom. I don't know what's taking him so long."

I scratched my cheek with the back of my thumb and said, "It's aight. I ain't got shit else do to."

I sat on the porch with my arms resting on my knees, watching Ryann give her weak ass nigga a hug before he climbed into his busted ass Impala to go to work as a fuckin' Uber driver. Broke ass corny nigga, yo. She deserved so much more. And I'm not talking about materialistic shit either.

Her boyfriend, he didn't lead the way he should. Ryann ran all over the cat. She wore the pants in their relationship. It was obvious. I took notice to that well before today. She got away with too much and been caught up in too much shit for him to still be fucking with her. Ryann must have some good ass pussy, but then again, ain't a pussy good enough in this world to make me play myself the way he was playing himself.

She slammed the car door and waved as he rode off. As soon as he was out of sight, she marched her thick ass back towards the house with a scowl on her face.

"What the fuck is your point—

Her cousin came back outside and interrupted her midsentence, "Here he comes, boo."

She sat next to me and I turned to her, "That's love, my baby. Good lookin'."

"Absolutely no problem," she blushed and looked up at Ryann and then back at me, "What you about to get into?"

"Hopefully you," I shot back, talking my shit, and ignoring the scowl on Ryann's face while she stood there with her arms crossed over her chest.

"Ashlee, take yo rat ass in the house, damn," said Ryann rolling her eyes.

She drew back, "Bitch, you green or what?"

"I thought you wanted to talk to Juice, nigga? Or are you now only interested in this bitch wettin' ya lil dick up," asked Ryann, purposely bumping into my head on her way up the stairs.

I chuckled and stood up, "Lil'? C'mon, sweetheart." I sucked my teeth and turned to who I now knew as Ashlee, "Say, Ashlee baby, you want to find out if this mafucka lil' or not?"

Ashlee licked her lips and said smirked, "I can find out now if you really about that shit."

35

Before anything else could be said, Juice walked out of the house, drying his hands on some paper towel. Ryann stormed passed him and pushed her way into the house. Juice's girlfriend followed after her.

Juice stepped down a couple of stairs and slapped hands with me, "Let's rap in the crib real fast."

"Bet," I said as I ignored the eye fucking Ashlee was giving me.

I wasn't interested in touching that bitch, let alone sticking dick to her. I just wanted to piss Ryann off and by the look on her face when I walked in the crib behind Juice, I had done just that.

"Damn Juice, you just letting anybody in this bitch? Did you forget that this was my house? And I don't want random ass niggas in my shit," she yelled as she jumped up from the couch.

"Sit yo ass down, Ry. This nigga ain't too much of a stranger, you takin gun charges and shit for 'eem," said Juice as we continued by him.

To my surprise, Ryann sat down, but that mug didn't leave her face. Fuck she so mad about, huh? Wasn't she just rubbing all up on her nigga? Probably sucked his dick and fucked 'em last night too, but she sitting there mad as fuck. Crazy.

Juice and I jogged down the stairs to the basement where it was set up like another crib. He flicked the light on and told me I could kick back on the couch. I decided to stand. I didn't want to get too comfortable. I was always on the defense, 'specially because I didn't know what this nigga wanted.

"What's good, bruh?" I asked him.

He fished a pack of cigarettes from his pocket and pulled one out before saying, "I need a you to front me some work."

I laughed. I literally cracked up laughing at him. But the nigga was dead ass serious. I could see the stress etched deeply in his face. He wasn't bullshitting and I couldn't believe it.

"Nigga, you's a murderer. The fuck you want some work for?"

He took a long pull from his cigarette and blew out a thick cloud of smoke, "Yo, you know I'm good for it—

I stuffed my hands in my pockets and interrupted him, "Don't give a fuck about what you good for, G. Like I said, you's a hitter. What you want work for? You want the favor. I need answers."

Shit just didn't sit right with me. I'm always on edge, wondering what's what and who's who. This nigga standing in front of me was Juice, the infamous hitman, but he's asking for work? That raised all kinds of red flags. Dawg asking for work and his sister just took a gun charge for me? Did them boys get to him? They want him to work for 'em or what? I could be wrong, but then again, I could be right.

"Bills piling in and works been a little," he made a *ssss* noise. "Light."

"Get with Chicago in a few days, he might have something for you," I told him. "Fuck you gone do with the work though, Juice? You never hustled a day in your life."

He shrugged, "Before I became who I am, I had never killed a mafucka either."

Ryann –

"That's perfect. Hold it right there," I said to the family of three who were beautifully posing for my camera.

It was a beautiful day, and we were shooting at Belle Isle, near the James Scott Memorial Fountain. The Johnsons were my third clients today and my absolute favorite. They had the prettiest little daughter and just looked to have everything together. While I photographed them, I wondered if I would ever have anything like this. I started to feel weird again, like there was something wrong with me for not being in love or having this by now. I'm twenty four, shit like this takes time to build. By time I'm ready to have kids, I'll be damn near thirty. I don't want to be one of those senior citizen ass mommas.

"Yes, absolutely gorgeous, Little Miss Daisy," I said to the daughter. She was the fuckin' cutest.

Mr. Johnson's eyes averted from my lens and his eyebrows snapped together.

"Is everything okay," I asked, noticing the sudden change in his disposition.

"Beautiful day for family portraits. Y'all look nice. Don't let me interrupt, please. Carry on."

My heart damn near exploded at the sound of his raspy voice. I licked my lips and slowly turned around. Cass was walking up behind me with his hands stuffed into the front pockets of his stone wash colored shorts. He had his dreads up into a high man-bun and his line-up was crisp. He looked good. Yummy as fuck, you hear me? I loved the way the thin fabric of his red v-neck shirt clung against his protruding muscles.

But I was mad at the nigga, so I sucked my teeth and rolled my eyes.

"I'm sorry Mr. and Mrs. Johnson; could you please give me just one moment?"

Mrs. Johnson nodded, "Take your time, Ryann."

They didn't seem bothered about the interruption, but he had me looking unprofessional as hell. I took my work serious and for him to pop up knowing that we aren't on good terms, just blew the fuck out of me.

He had the nerve to be smiling as I treaded towards him, "You look astounding, sweetheart. So damn fine, Mr. Johnson can't seem to keep his eyes off that juicy mafucka you luggin' around. He's lucky I'm in a good mood today."

I narrowed my eyes at him, "I'm working."

He nodded, "I can see that, gorgeous. We need to rap once you finish up."

I pulled my lips into my mouth and sighed. I was mad, but I couldn't deny the heavy beating of my heart. Nor my pulsating pussy. But he pissed me off so bad last night that I didn't even want to be around him. I was straight smooth on his rude ass.

"I don't associate with fake mafuckas."

"Thank God I'm the realest nigga living," he cockily replied with a smirk on his face.

"Fuck on... you about as fake as they come."

He rose his eyebrows, "Is that right?"

"Yes, it is. Have a good day, Cass."

"I will," he said before turning to walk away.

That was easier than I expected. And I'm happy he just walked his black ass off. I did not want to be out here cutting up in front of these boujee ass black people.

*

After I finished shooting the Johnsons, my stomach started to rumble like crazy. I had been out since early this morning and only had a bagel. I woke up late and had to hurry out of the door. So, I'm running off a large coffee and a damn bagel. I began to pack up and then headed over to my car. As soon as I got to my car, I realized why Cass had walked off so easily.

He pushed himself up off the hood of the car and headed over to me, "Let me get that for you, sweetheart."

I pressed my lips together and then told him I that I was good and didn't need his help. He ignored me and grabbed the backpack out of my hands anyway.

"I need the key out of that front pocket," I said to him as he stood there, waiting for me to unlock the doors.

He fished my keys from the front pocket of my backpack and then tossed them to me. I hit the unlock button and he put my bag in the backseat. Then he boldly walked to the other side of the car and hopped in the passenger seat.

I stood outside of the car running my hands over my hair, sighing. This nigga really pissed me off last night. I couldn't believe the shit he said to Ashlee. Like, my blood was boiling, no lie. I'd like to smack the piss out of both of them. This nigga for slick talking to my cousin and that bitch for blushing and practically begging to swallow his dick.

I knew he was being petty, mad because I was posted up with Dinero. Mad because I didn't link with him that night. I mean, what the fuck? I am in a relationship and he knows that.

"You gone get in? Or you gone stand out there pretending like you're not happy to see me?" said Cass, looking over the car at me.

I shook my head and got inside. There was so much I wanted to say. But his cologne crept up into my nostrils, suffocating me, making me lose my voice, making me lose bits and pieces of myself along with it.

"You aight?" he asked.

I didn't realize that I had closed my eyes and was intensely gripping the steering wheel. Thoughts of what he said to Ashlee had evaded my mind again, putting me at my highest point of pissitivity. And just like that, I had a voice.

"Nah, I'm not aight. What the fuck do you think, nigga? Why are you even here? Shouldn't you be laid up with Ashlee right now?" I asked with flaring nostrils, steady squeezing the steering wheel.

"Who?" he asked with furrowed eyebrows. "Fuck is Ashlee...oh you talm 'bout girl I was talking mess to yesterday? Man, I was just talkin."

"Just talkin," I said with a chuckle. "Just fuckin' talkin?! Nigga..." I took a deep breath, realizing that I was tripping. Like, seriously tripping. I was sitting there talking to him like he was my nigga. In my mind, he was. But hell, he didn't know that and I was probably looking like a looney tune type bitch right now. So, I dialed back. "I'm tripping."

"A lil bit," he said as he pulled his seatbelt on. "Like you wasn't practically fuckin' ya cornball ass nigga right there on the porch. But it's cool though. You got some learning to do. We gone work on that."

I giggled, "Fucking him? Cass, I was sitting on his lap."

His eyes met mine and he said, "His hands, his mouth...none of that shit should ever even touch you, period. You need to dead shit with that clown, like, right now."

And I thought I was the one tripping. He wanted me to just leave my relationship for him. My infatuation with him made me want to. But it would be stupid as hell for me to just up and leave my relationship for a man I don't even know. I wasn't the happiest with Dinero, but I was comfortable. I knew him.

Things were straight between Dinero and I. He was starting to be around too much though. I knew it was because he was worried about Cass and I, but got damn he was annoying me. A bitch needed some space, but he was suffocating me and not in the way being around Cass did. In a way that made me never want to be around him.

I switched the subject and said, "What are you doing up here anyway?"

He licked his lips, "Looking for you."

"How did you know I would be here?"

"I can't keep my eyes off you, Ms. Ryann," he said with a half smile like he didn't just admit to basically stalking me.

I mean, I couldn't get mad. I was legit stalking him on the regular.

"You serious about what you do. I fucks with it. You get some good shots," he asked, nodding towards my camera on my neck.

"Just work stuff," I said as I cranked the engine up.

"What about your personal stuff?" he asked while buckling his seat belt.

"Didn't do that today," I quickly said. "What's up?"

I didn't want him asking anything about my personal stuff. I have memory cards full of pictures of him. I never, ever, wanted him to know about that. I was taking that to my grave.

But what about when I die? Oh lawd, people will find out. My nosey ass family will definitely go through my photos. And I'm quite sure I'll die married to this black mafucka sitting next to me. He's going to miss me like crazy and want to look through pictures and shit, to reminisce about my fine ass. What will happen when he comes across my collection of pictures of him? Will he stop loving me? What will he think? A bitch has got to figure this shit out. I cannot be out here looking like a creep. I mean, I'll be dead but I don't want that to be my legacy. The fuck?

Cass's voice snapped me out of my little trance, "I'm hungry. Do you eat?"

"Duh," I said with my feistiness. "Do you?"

"Depends on what's on the menu," he shot back, catching my little slick talk.

I blushed and looked away, "Where you trying to eat at?"

"It's up to you, sweetheart. We can keep it basic or if you one of them high sidity women, we can go that route too. The decision is yours. You can have whatever you like."

What else can I have? Can I have you? For just one night, or the rest of my life perhaps? Whichever you prefer. But, Lord knows I want you.

My soul craved for his black royalty looking ass, sitting next to me, gawking over at me with those soul-seeking eyes of his. His eye contact was insane. He looked at me as if he was actually looking inside of me. I swear, I don't think I've ever had anybody look at me with such passion behind their eyes.

"I'm not hard to please," I said as I fumbled around with the AC.

"Is that right," he asked.

I swallowed and nodded, feeling myself grow hotter although the air was blowing in my face. It was Cass. It was always Cass.

"Mmhmm," I quickly replied. This conversation had gone from innocent to dirty in the matter of seconds. Hell, were we even still talking about food? I licked my lips and let out a deep breath, trying not to let my infatuation with him take over the way it usually does.

"Come on, Cass, where you trying to eat, man?" I asked with a slight chuckle as I placed hair behind my ear.

"Mama's," he said with a hint of sarcasm in his voice.

I snapped my head in his direction. How did he know I liked Mama's? Okay... this shit was starting to be a little creepy. I mean, yeah, I take pictures, but this nigga don't know that. He's blatantly putting it out there that he's been watching me. Not one fuck has been given on his end either.

But we couldn't eat at Mama's. Too many people who knew Dinero and I went there.

"How do you know I eat at Mama's?"

He shrugged and ran his tongue over his bottom lip, "Who don't eat at Mama's?"

I twisted my lips up in a 'yeah, okay' fashion and pulled off, "I'm not going all the way over there. Tim Horton's right down the street."

I expected him to turn Tim Horton's down, but he relaxed in his seat and said, "Tim Horton's it is."

*

The chemistry was undeniable. As I sat across from Cass, I couldn't believe how perfectly things were going. The crazy nervousness I'd usually get around him had subsided a bit and I was thoroughly enjoying myself. Enjoying myself like I didn't have a man at my house waiting for me to come home.

He had text me a dozen times, wondering where I was. The last time I text him I told him that I was finishing up my final shoot, although I had finished almost two hours ago. I didn't realize so much time had passed until I sent him that message. Time flew when you're having fun. I hadn't smiled so genuinely nor blushed so hard in my life. Cass had a way with words that'd make a nun drop her draws.

"When will I see you again?" I asked Cass as I pulled up behind his Benz.

We were back at Belle Isle. Our little lunch date was over and I was sad about it.

"Whenever you want to see me. All you gotta do is call," he said staring me in the eyes.

That's another thing I adored about Cass. His eye contact was always direct. Never wavering like he was searching for a lie to tell. Through his eye contact, I could see the truth.

I chewed on my bottom lip as I ignored yet another call from Dinero.

Cass nodded towards my phone, "You can have me all of the time if you get rid of that inconvenience."

I looked away, out of the window, "I know."

Cass grabbed my hand from the steering wheel and a shock transferred between us causing me to slightly flinch.

"What are you so afraid of, Ryann?" asked Cass.

I swallowed and tried to control the heavy beating of my heart.

"Yo," he said after I sat there quiet, possibly for too long.

"Change," I blurted out.

"To live is to change, sweetheart."

I shifted uncomfortably in my seat, "Yeah, I know."

"Stepping outside of ya comfort zone will be the best decision you've ever made in ya life."

There was that certainty again. The same certainty he had in his voice the day he promised me the cop wouldn't hurt me. Like he knew what he said was true and like I had no other choice but to believe him. And just like that day, I did believe him.

*

It's crazy how your mood can switch up as soon as you enter an environment you don't want to be in. I was all smiles and butterflies before I came back to the hood, but, as soon as I did, my mood went left.

"Ya man been lookin for you for hours, bitch," said Ashlee as soon as I climbed the stairs to the house with a smirk on her face. "He was about to send a search team out lookin' for yo lying ass."

"Bitch, he knew where I was at. I been textin' him. Where he at," I asked.

"Where you left his sorry ass," she said with a giggle. "Aye you got twenty I can borrow—

"This morning you wanted condoms, now you asking for money? Damn, bitch, is there ever a time you don't need anything," I snapped.

I was mad because Dinero was still at my house. I should have known he was still here by the way he was texting and calling me. I wanted him the fuck gone. I already knew there was an argument waiting for me on the other side of the door. An argument I did not have the energy for.

"I'm trying to go scoop Shaneka up, you fake ass ho," said Ashlee before storming down the stairs.

I felt bad.

"Aw shit. My bad, LeeLee. I'll go pick her up," I yelled as she carried on down the block. She flipped me the bird and kept walking. "Why didn't you just say that, damn?!"

I sighed and walked into the house, feeling pretty shitty for taking my annoyance out on her. As soon as I stepped foot into the living room, I wanted to explode even further. My house was a mess. There were three plates on my coffee table, a cup, crumbs all over the carpet and table, and my couch pillows were thrown all about. Ashlee is a fairly clean person, so I knew she didn't do it. Definitely not. This mess had Dinero written all over it.

Stepping into the kitchen, I'd like to fuck some shit up. The kitchen was a complete mess, do you hear me? Dishes piled into the sink and there were a few skillets sitting on my stove covered in caked on residue from whatever he cooked. He left my carton of orange juice out, in addition to cheese, milk, and eggshells. He can live however he pleases at that nasty ass apartment in midtown, but when it comes to my house he will respect it.

I stormed down the hall to my bedroom and pushed the door open. He had the nerve to be laid in my bed, scrolling through his phone like he didn't have a mess to clean up.

"Get up and clean that shit up, D. I am not playing—"

"Wouldn't be a mess if you woulda brought a nigga back something to eat. Where you been, Ry? You only had three gigs today. Yet, you've been gone for over six hours."

I pulled the sheet off his body and screamed, "Go clean my fuckin' house up, Dinero! This ain't that, my baby!"

I was so heated. He was really blaming the mess he made on me. Really? Fuckin really?

"Typical Ryann," said Dinero with a chuckle. "You get caught up in some shit and trip out."

"No nigga, I'm spazzing because when I left my house it was clean. Cleeean. So please, get your ass up and go clean that shit up," I said, moving my hand in a 'hurry up' gesture.

"Tell me where you were, Ryann," he said staring at me.

My top lip curled up into a frown and I walked away to put my camera away, "I was working. You know this already, my nigga. Man, I'm getting about tired of you always questioning me about shit. The fuck? I caught the neighborhood rat climbing out of your Imp and I've been chill."

"Because it was for work. I have every right—

"If you don't trust me, leave me."

I was talking like I really wasn't out at basic ass Tim Horton's with Cass for two hours having more fun with him than I've had with Dinero in months.

He moved down to the end of the bed and then stood up, naked as the day he was born, "I'm trying to trust you baby, but damn, you makin it hard."

Why was he naked? I wouldn't care if when I left he was naked, but he wasn't. When I left he had on basketball shorts.

"Why you laid up naked, D?" I asked turning around to face him. "You fuck Ashlee?"

I was tripping. My insecurities were brought on by my own infidelities.

"Man, gone on with that shit. I'm naked because I took a shower and wanted to let my nuts hang freely in this bitch. Hopin that when my girl got back I could fuck."

I shook my head and pushed him away. He stood behind me with his dick pressed against me. I wasn't even feeling it. This trifling ass nigga had left my house a complete mess. He was trying to throw me off with the insecure talk and sex. I just wanted him to clean his mess up and go home.

"Straight up, Ry? You pushing me away?"

"My house is a mess. Put it back the way you found it, D."

Dinero stepped off, scratching the side of his face. He grabbed his shorts off the chair next to my bed and slipped them on, "Aight, aight. Yo, I was thinking," he began as he pulled his shirt over his head. "We been goin through it heavy as hell lately. You want to go to couples counseling? I think that shit with Tiny been really messing with you."

"I'm not into putting people in my business, D. It's not that serious, calm down. I'm not worried about Tiny—trust me."

He approached me and wrapped his arms around me, "I just want my Ryann back."

She was gone and he was forcing it. Every day, I got closer and closer to leaving him. But there was a small voice in the back of my mind that told me that he wasn't going to make it easy. Clearly Dinero was emotionally unstable. He wanted this relationship to work too bad to just let me break up with him. I might have to shoot his ass or something.

"I'm cool," I replied.

He kissed the nape of my neck and let me go, heading to clean his mess up.

"Make sho' you use that Dawn too," I said jokingly just to kill the depressed vibe he was giving off. "Don't use no damn bar of soap, Dinero."

He chuckled and said, "Ahh, you got jokes."

*

"This bitch a gangsta now," I joked as I pushed Shaneka down the hall in the wheelchair she was being discharged in. "She done took a slug!"

She giggled and looked over her shoulder at me, "Girl, bye!"

Ashlee sucked her teeth, "Let me push her, Ry."

I frowned and looked over at her, "You play too much, bitch. You can't be pushing her all wild like that. She ain't fully recovered."

Shaneka was finally coming home, and to be honest, I wasn't sure if that was a good or bad thing. She would require a lot of care and Ashlee just ain't dependable. I felt like I was about to have my hands full with Nek. I didn't really mind, it's just that, I have shit to do. I have wedding gigs lined up for the next three weekends, plus a few family's to shoot. Meanwhile, Ashlee does nothing but run the hood getting high and drunk all day. With all of that free time, I bet she still didn't look out the way she's supposed to. I'm sure auntie won't mind coming to take care of Nek, but she and my uncle had moved to Ohio after the last incident with Boo and Henny.

"You talked to your momma, Shaneka," I asked as we got onto the elevator.

"Yeah, she said she's visiting," she replied.

"Good. I need some damn money. My phone bill due. When she say she coming?" asked Ashlee with her back against the wall of the elevator.

"How is it that yo ass always broke, but you fuck with a ton of niggas," I asked with a slight laugh.

"I ain't no prostitute, bitch," she shot back.

"Might as well put a price tag on the pussy for all the millage you putting on that nasty mafucka," I replied just as the elevator doors opened.

She pointed her finger in my face, "Don't' worry about the miles on my pussy. What you should be worried about is who about to make them miles go up. Ya hear me?"

We walked off the elevator and I huffed. She was trying me, wasn't she? She was taking another little jab at Cass again. She's been having a field day throwing that little petty flirting he was doing with her in my face. To be honest, I wasn't sure if Ashlee really was trying to fuck him or get me to admit to feeling him. Whatever the case may be, she was about ten seconds away from getting dragged all around this fucking hospital.

"I sure didn't miss the arguing," said Shaneka with her hand to her head. "I might go back to Ohio with my ma and them."

For the sake of Nek's comfort, I piped down.

"Sorry Nek. Yo sister just wants me to beat her the fuck up, that's all."

"Girl, you know she's not going to mess with Dinero," said Shaneka, so out of the loop.

She didn't know about anything going on. To her knowledge, Dinero and I were still off and she hadn't a clue about what's been going on with Cass and I.

Ashlee sucked her teeth, "Dinero? Bitch, fuck Dinero. I'm talking about the nigga she scared to cheat on him with—Cass."

Shaneka's head whipped around so fast, I thought she would break her damn neck for sure.

"Dark skin Cass with the dreads? Ugly? The dope boy?"

"Dark skin Cass with the dreads," I nodded. "Ugly? Nah. Dope boy? That is him."

"Oh," she said before turning back around. "Girl, you better leave him alone."

"Why'd you say that?" I asked, taking notice to the switch up of her demeanor.

She shrugged, "I'm just saying."

- Cass -

"That's Cass," I heard somebody yell over the loud music blasting from the speakers sitting by the pool.

I pulled my Buff's down from my head and placed them over my eyes. A nigga was dead ass tired of hearing my name. Every room I moved to, I heard the shit. How was it that I had to be the most anti-social person at this bitch, yet everybody knew me? Or wanted to know me. Lil' slut bitches with hot pussies wanting to hop on my dick because of who I was.

If I didn't have this money, if I wasn't pushing a beamer, Benz, and Bentley, if I didn't run the streets of the east side of Detroit, these bitches would pay me no mind. If I wasn't sitting here draped in designer, rocking a pair of Buffs, I would be invisible. If I was the same bum ass nigga I was before I got my hands on that dope, they would walk by with their noses turned up.

You know why? Because without the money, I was just another average nigga with dreads. Straight facts. I know what it is and I couldn't really give a fuck less either. I never took any of these bitches serious because of that fact alone. I could see through all of the fake smiles and forced conversations. None of 'em was genuine. Well, all but one.

But shorty...she didn't even fit in the category these sluts fit in. She was in a lane of her own. Ryann. Ms. Ryann, the photographer. She was a rare gem in a pile full of foggy ass rhinestones.

"Hey Cass," said someone, sitting next to the beach lounger I sat on.

"What's good," I replied.

"Why you sitting over here by yourself? You're not going to get in the pool?" she asked.

I couldn't describe the bitch to you if I wanted to. I hadn't looked at her, and because of such, she took it upon herself to sit on the same lounger I was kicked back on, right at my feet.

She sucked her teeth, "Cass? Did you hear me? I said why aren't you swimming—"

"Fuck I look like swimming in a pool full of people I don't know shit about? Mafuckas prolly pissin all in that shit. Yet, y'all steady dippin' yall heads in that shit. Swimming in piss and other peoples dirt."

She giggled, "Oh my God. There's chlorine—"

"What's good, shorty? You need some weed? Wavy got bud on em," I said cutting her off again.

I was only here because I was invited. Today was Luck's son's birthday. Lil' Dawg was turning five. Crazy as shit how it was crowded with more half naked sluts than it was kids. A bunch of thot ass single moms who really only came because they knew Luck ran with a squad of money getting niggas. On the top of that list? Me.

I was looked at as an easy ticket. A get out of the hood free ticket. But I was so lowkey with my shit that they didn't know I was the wrong nigga to come at with that cutesy shit. I wasn't fazed by it.

"Noooo," she said dragging the word out. "I was just wanting to you know...talk to you."

"How many kids you got runnin around here?" I asked, finally taking my glasses off my face to get a good look at her.

She looked up, counting I guess, "Five—

"Where are they? Shouldn't you be focused on keepin' ya eyes on ya starting lineup, darling?"

I put my feet flat on the ground and stood up. I was about ten seconds from giving Nate his birthday gift and dipping.

"They alright," she said waving towards the pool. "They swimming."

I squinted at her and then walked away. I prayed to God he watched over my dick and the decisions he made. I never wanted to fuck around and slip up in a bitch like the ones I've been encountering lately. No one gave a damn about their kids. They were so wrapped up in living, that they paid their kids no attention. My nigga Luck and his girl... they were the only parents I knew that had sense. Aside from the hood rats, the party was nice. Luck had a clown come out, they had about five bounce houses, cotton candy machines, face painting... the whole nine. Nate was one happy kid.

I didn't know if my sympathy for kids came from my fucked up upbringing or what, but I'm sure it played a major part. Like I said before, the youth were really all I cared about. I didn't give a fuck about myself...but kids? I gave a damn about the kids.

My phone chimed and I fished it from my shorts. There was a picture of the sunrise with the text: *my best capture today.* Since Ryann and I've been kicking it, she's been sending me her best picture of the day, par my request. This one was my favorite yet.

I texted her back: *You want to watch it set with a nigga?*

And Ryann. In addition to the kids, I cared about Ryann.

I can try, she texted back. I gritted my teeth and stuffed my phone back into my pocket.

I cared about her. But was it enough to stick around while she entertained another nigga? I didn't give a fuck that she was trying to sort through shit. I didn't give a flyin' fuck about her not wanting to ruini a friendship. Shit was dead ass just an excuse to me. I would have been stopped fuckin' with Ryann a long time ago, but she made me move in ways I've never been moved in before. You see she got me wanting to watch the sun set and shit. I've never done that. Never cared too. But because she cared about all things beautiful, I wanted to care about it too. On top of that, she was a thoroughbred in a world full of frauds. I was seriously digging baby, but I was about over her nigga being in the picture.

"You gone, bro?" I heard Luck call out.

I looked over my shoulder and he was jogging up behind me wearing his party hat cocked to the side.

"Roll 'lat weed up, pussy," I said as I tossed a jar of good ass green to him as soon as he got to me.

He made an ugly face after cracking it open and sniffing it, "Shit G. This that new-new? Straight fye!"

I nodded with a smile on my face, "You know what it is. Roll it the fuck up, bruhhh."

"Copy that," he said as he tucked it into the pocket of his button up Polo. "Let's hit the cave real quick wit it."

I nodded, "Where all the kids at, G? This bitch flooded with a bunch of basic broke broads looking for a quick meal."

Luck snorted and laughed, "Sinn's hood rat ass friends. Soon as they heard Cass was gone be in the building they all slid through. Most of 'em ain't even got kids."

"Wild," I replied as I slid the patio doors open. "Girl not comin' through is she?"

Luck looked over his shoulder at me, "Now you know sis swinging through."

I shook my head, "I'm definitely about to skate on that note then."

Luck's girlfriend has this sister named Symone. The four of us—Luck, Sinn, Symone, and me—use to hang tough. Sinn and Luck were a couple, so granted Symone and me had a thing going on too. She was my first piece of pussy. As expected, I wasn't her first piece of dick. She had a higher advantage, being the pretty chick with the fat ass. Me? I was just a broke ass, nappy headed, funny lookin' nigga. Symone rocked with me regardless, though. She was down from the bottom and til this day, I've always appreciated that. Unfortunately, shit flipped when I hit the top.

As soon as I started to see real cheese off this drug shit, everything changed. I wasn't in love with her, but she was falling for me. I never got too close to people because shit, I didn't see the need to. Who in this world could really give a damn about me if my own parents didn't? I had trust issues. And since I had trust issues, I didn't commit to her. For the fuck what? The thing we had going on...it wasn't a relationship. We were just mad cool and fucked around on the regular.

But when that money started to flood in, bitches came out the woodwork. I won't front, it was something different for me and I appreciated the attention and pussy that came with it. Symone was busy trying to lock me down, but all I wanted to do was enjoy life. We ended on bad terms because she couldn't let go of feelings she acquired on her own.

"I heard she got engaged though, bruh," said Luck.

I turned my mouth down with a nod, "Good for her."

I wasn't being funny or shit like that neither. Symone is a good woman and will make a good wife. I was happy for baby girl, still didn't want to be around the bitch though. She was a good woman indeed, but she had a mean streak like none other. She hated me and I couldn't blame her.

My phone rung and I fished it from my pocket again. It was Ryann. I slid the phone over and answered for her.

"Wassup, gorgeous?"

"How you gon' say something about watching the sunset then stop texting. Where's the consistency," she jokingly asked.

"You want to watch the shit with me? Or you worried about sneaking away from ya weak ass nigga?" I asked, getting straight to the point.

"Cass—

"Ryann, I understand ya guilt and all 'lat. But I told you, sweetheart, time is of essence and you wasting a lot of it. Mine included, to be completely real, shorty."

There was brief moment of silence before she finally said something, "What time you gone be in the hood, nigga?"

I laughed, "Around six thirty. Don't wear them ugly ass slides neither."

We joked around a little bit before we ended our conversation. Shorty put a thorough ass smile on my face whenever I heard her voice. Not too many woman—if ever any—had that effect on me. I can keep it a stack, she had me open a lil' bit. Had ya boy sending out good morning texts and all that, on some regular nigga shit.

Me and Luck jogged down the basement stairs and sat on the leather couch.

Luck pulled a back wood from his pocket and asked, "You fuck with shorty heavy, huh? She official?"

I nodded, "Baby took a gun charge for a nigga she don't even know. A lil' nutty, but she official."

"How long y'all been kickin it, G," he asked.

I thought for a moment, "'Bout three weeks. Why?"

He opened the jar of weed and looked over at me, "Shorty still fuckin' with that cur ass Uber driver?"

I smirked and said, "Stop askin questions and roll that weed up, G."

I was snappy when it came to mentioning that nigga. It wasn't a jealousy thing—shit no it wasn't. Every time she's with that goofy, it's me who she wants to be with.

*

I looked down at my phone and shook my head. Twenty minutes in the hood and Ryann ain't text or called a nigga back. Fuck it. You try to introduce a mafucka to something different, but they too wrapped up in mediocrity to step outside of the box. I bet money she's gone come at me with a bogus ass excuse later. Talm'bout she'll try to get away from her fuck ass nigga, meanwhile, she's prolly over there bending over, letting him stick dick to her.

My nostrils slightly flared at the thought of him violating pussy that will eventually belong to me. I felt like a sucka ass nigga sitting here waiting on a text and a call. Fuck 'er though.

"Hey Cass," said some thot in the trap, kicking it with Wavy and a few other niggas I had on pay roll.

I nodded and leaned my head back on the couch cushion, about ready to say fuck it all and dip out.

She scooted closer to me and crossed one leg over the other, "You okay?"

"You here for Wavy and them right?" I asked, uninterested in conversation.

She giggled, "I could be here for you though. Would that be okay?"

"Nah," I pushed myself up from the couch and headed to the back of the house where them niggas stood around passing a blunt back and forth between each other.

I could spot a cheese eater from a mile away. Like I said before, any time a bitch comes up to me on some hey Cass type shit, I already know what it is. Especially the ones with a bad rep as is. I didn't know girl, but she was chillin in a trap for fucks sake. That there told me all I needed to know.

"Go grab ya bitch," I said, leaning up against the sink.

Wavy chuckled and puffed from the blunt twice before passing it to me. He then walked out of the kitchen.

"Ay bro, we about to toss this bitch around. You don't want in on the pussy?" asked Nino.

I pulled from the blunt and passed it back to him, "Shit no. Have fun with that, though."

If I needed my dick wet, I could call any one of the broads in my contacts. I didn't partake in the gay type shit these niggas were into. At this present moment, I wanted to be sticking dick to Ryann, but she was too busy bending over for another nigga. Prolly got her lips wrapped around his dick right now, while I'm over here waiting on a weak ass text.

"Yo you sure—

"Fuck I just say to you, nigga?" I snapped.

I was snapping on him because I couldn't get the image of Ryann making fuck faces for another nigga out of my head. Never have I ever been this interested in a woman. There was something different about her that made me feel in ways that I couldn't shake. I needed to have her in my life and it had been decades since I needed a damn soul.

Nino held his hands up, "Aight bro."

On my way out of the kitchen, I could hear the bitch moaning and yelling. Couple minutes ago, she was just pushing up on me, trying to sweet talk me with the same mouth she's in the room she's sucking dick with. Ho's man. Ho's are the exact reason why my trust is so screwed up now. Because of how quickly she switched up, I never did anything but fuck 'em. That's all they wanted anyway and all I wanted from them in return. But from Ryann, I wanted more. I wanted to get to know her in and out. The more she curved, me the more I thought maybe I was wasting my time.

"Ohhhh... Please Cass come fuck me," the girl in the room getting a train ran on her moaned.

"Yo, what the fuck?" I said as I got ready to leave.

"Mmmh, come fuck my pussy Cass," she moaned.

Chicago walked into the trap and slapped hands with me, "Yo, what the fuck is that about?" He was cracking up, but I didn't find anything funny. Shit was straight up creepy.

I walked off and kicked the bedroom door open. Wavy flinched and she hopped off his dick, eager to grab my shorts to lower them.

I smacked her hands away, "Stop callin' me and shit, bitch. Shit's mad weird. Mouth full of dick, yet Cass still coming out of that mafucka."

She stared up at me with tears streaming down her face, "Fuck you."

"Yeah, you want to, but I don't want that funky snatch. Type bitch let a team of niggas beat with her pussy on yuck?"

She started to say something else, but I walked off. Room full of niggas fucking a bitch with rotten pussy.

*

"Hey, you leaving?"

I looked over my shoulder at Ryann crossing the street.

I looked up to the sky, "Sun already set."

She wrapped her arms around her body and stood in front of me, "So?"

I looked down at her pretty face, wondering why I couldn't shake these feelings I had for her. I didn't feel. I was numb when it came to women, but I felt shit with her. And the fucked up part about all of this was that she was someone elses.

"So...you gone handle yo fuckin' situation or what, ma? I'm not a fuckin' side nigga Ryann. When I tell you I want to watch the sun set with you, I expect to watch it. Not sit around watchin my phone like a bitch. Stop playin' with me, my baby. Either you rockin' or you not."

She ran her hand over the back of her head and looked down the block. Lil' nigga named Peewee was riding up with his fat ass side kick. Peewee is her boyfriend's lil' brother. She looked like she'd seen a ghost when he rode by shaking his head with a smirk on his face.

I huffed, and hopped in the whip, then cranked the engine up. Before I could scur off, she knocked on the window.

I rolled it down, "Gone back across the street, sweetheart. Shit was smooth while it lasted—

"Can I tell you why at least, Cass?" she said. She looked up to the sky, "It's about to rain."

"Get in."

She hurried to the passenger side of the car and climbed in.

"Strap up," I said nodding towards the seat belt.

She did and I pulled off.

If Ryann was anyone else, I would have pulled off on her ass. Would have left her standing in the middle of the block to get rained on. Even knowing that she lived right across the street and could easily run into the crib for shelter from the rain, I wanted to get her from up under the dark sky. I didn't want rain to hit her. I cared about shit like her hair getting ruined, or her clothes getting wet. I cared about her too much.

"Thought you wanted to talk," I said after about five minutes of silence.

"My parents were murdered by a drug dealer," she said with her hands in between her legs, which were bouncing rapidly.

"Fuck," I said as I dragged my freehand down over my mouth.

- Ryann -

I looked out of the window at the rain pouring down, while Cass's hand sat upon my thigh. I just told him why. Why I couldn't leave Dinero just to jump into a relationship with him. I could tell that he was starting to think that I was conflicted because I was in love with Dinero, but that was the furthest thing from the truth.

Dinero and I only shared a title. Cass and I...we shared something much deeper. In such a short period of time, infatuation had blossomed into love, or at least that is what it felt like.

With Cass, I could envision a future. I imagined starting a family. I wanted that Cinderella type wedding. But then there was that barrier. That one thing that stood in the way. His title. His lifestyle. Sometimes, when I was so wrapped up in the fantasy I called Cass, that I could see past the life he lived. But then shit would pop off and I would be reminded of why to stay away.

Just the other day, one of the niggas that worked for him were shot in the head. That could have been Cass. And when I told him this, he looked at me, laughed and asked me if I knew who it was that I was fuckin with. That cocky shit that drove me crazy. He walked around like he was invincible. Good God, how I wish he was. But he was not. And because he wasn't, I couldn't give him that title. I couldn't call him my boyfriend. To be honest, a title wasn't even needed. But a title would make it real.

Three weeks had gone by. And within those three weeks, I'd fallen in love. It had to be love. Speaking and being with Cass was the highlight of my day. Before, taking pictures was. And even then, it was taking pictures of him that made my day. Now it was just to hear his voice, or to feel his skin against mine. If I didn't see Cass, my day would be off. So when he threatened to leave me, I felt lost and he hadn't even driven away yet. Anxiety had begun to creep upon me so before it could sat in, I stopped him before he could go.

Because I didn't want to lose him, I told him my truth. I hadn't told him the whole truth. I hadn't told him that I found my parents dead. I didn't tell him that it was because of their death that I had my .380 on me as we spoke. I felt like it might be too soon for the whole truth. But he needed it. It was necessary. For without it, I felt like I would be without him. And I couldn't have that.

"Ryann," said Cass as he moved his hand back and forth over my exposed thigh.

The weather had gone from nice to shitty all within an hour's span. Before the sunset, it was beautiful. I wonder if I would have made our date to watch the sunset, if it would be raining right now. It was almost as if God was crying tears because I was allowing my fear to stand in the way of destiny.

Dinero wouldn't leave. Not until I gave him some pussy. He was all over me, begging me. I was trying everything in my power to get him to go to work. I hated that Uber was so flexible and that he could work when he wanted to. I tried to create an argument, I tried to lie and say that Omni wanted to link...and all of that. But he wouldn't stop. He wanted me. Eventually, I gave in and not only to get rid of him, but because he was eating my pussy mercilessly to a point where I couldn't protest.

He left right after showering. And as soon as he did, I hopped into the shower myself. I scrubbed my body in disgust and hurried outside in the nick of time.

"Huh?" I asked as I tore my eyes away from the pouring of the rain.

"I asked if you wanted to talk about it."

"I don't want to. But I need to," I honestly told him. "Can you pull over? I hate driving in the rain."

He nodded and pulled over into the parking lot of a grocery store. He killed the engine and adjusted his seat before saying, "Come here."

I looked over at his lap, hesitant. I've never sat on his lap and I wondered if I would be able to. Lately, I hadn't been as nervous as before around him. But sitting on his lap would be different. I would feel parts of him I had yet to touch. I didn't know if I could handle that.

Cass interrupted my thoughts by unbuckling my seatbelt and pulling me on his lap.

I froze up and he told me to breath.

I closed my eyes and allowed air to fill my lungs.

"I've never had a woman act this way before," he said as he wrapped his arms around my body.

You've never had a woman adore you as much as I adore you, that's why. Is what I wanted to say, but instead I said nothing. He would probably think I was crazy. How could I feel this way about him within this short period of time? He wouldn't be able to understand that this infatuation started well before we made eye contact. Well before he noticed me sitting on the porch in my ugly ass slides as he likes to call them. Oh no, this infatuation started when snow still fell from the sky.

I giggled and looked away with a shrug.

"I don't know how to respond to it, sweetheart," he admitted. "If I'm ever overstepping boundaries or making you uncomfortable, let me know. A niggas not trying to be on any rapey shit."

I furrowed my eyebrows and said, "You respond perfectly. I just... I don't know... this is new to me too, Cass."

"If I kissed you would I be overstepping boundaries?" he asked before licking his lips.

"There aren't any boundaries for you to overstep," I said with my eyes on his full lips.

Kiss me.

Touch me.

Fuck me.

I wanted it all from Cass. When he inched in closer to me, my breathing got labored and my heart rate picked up. My body responded to him in ways I've never experienced. I wanted his lips on me so bad. I wanted to know if they were as soft as they looked.

And they were.

When his lips met mine, tingles shot through my body and the world began to spin.

It was a sweet, wet kiss with no tongue, but it held so much passion.

We both pulled away from the kiss at the same time and I shied away with a blush. This nigga made me feel like a giddy ass little girl.

"Soft as satin," said Cass with a half-smile.

I laughed, "Whatever."

He pulled me into his chest and said, "You ready to talk?"

"Yes," I managed to say.

My nerves were through the roof, but I did it.

I spilled my guts out to him. I told him every single detail about the day my parents were killed, with tears spilling from my eyes. Cass sat there, rubbing my back, letting me talk until I was finished.

He misunderstood my fear though. He thought I had something against dope boys solely because my parents were killed by one. No, that wasn't it. Every day, I had to live with the fear of losing one of my brothers, I did not want to live with the fear of losing Cass too.

Do you have any idea how much losing him would damage me? My shutter wouldn't sound. The world would be dark and dull if I didn't have photographing him to look forward to. If I couldn't stare into the emptiness of his dark eyes...if I was only left with a photo to stare at...it would kill me. I would die inside. The risks behind him being a dope boy petrified me just as much as my brothers being hitmen did.

Why couldn't these niggas live normal lives like Dinero? Why couldn't Cass be regular? Why did he have to be a dope boy with murderous tendencies? What happened to holding down a regular nine to five? What's so hard about that? If he could do that for me, we could be. But Cass... he wasn't a regular dude. Boring didn't suit his personality and I could tell by the look in his eyes that hustling was something he couldn't live without. It seemed like it was his passion, just as much as photography was mine.

But if photography was truly my passion, why would things change if I loss him, right? Because the moment Cass stepped into my crosshairs it all changed. Everything about photography. Everything about my life. It all changed. And since we've become something, life could never go back to the way it was before him. Things could never return to the way they were before I fell in love with his blackness.

"It's not that you sell drugs, Cass," I said as I looked at my manicured fingernails.

"What is it then?" he asked, grabbing hold of my chin, propping my head back so that I could stare into the black pearls that were called pupils.

"Death. The way that shit ends... I can't... if I lose you, I would lose me."

I couldn't believe how honest I was being with him. I had to be if I wanted to keep him. If I wanted him to understand why. I had to be open in order to save myself the heartbreak of being without him. If I didn't tell him the truth, he would stop talking to me and I couldn't have that. I couldn't just go back to not talking to him. Not after I've felt those butter soft lips upon mine. Not after I've felt his calloused hands on my body. Not after this intimacy. I couldn't admire such beauty from afar after witnessing it up close.

"You can't escape death, darlin'."

I shuddered at the thought of life without him, "You don't get it."

"Nah, I understand completely. But listen, sweetheart, ya cornball ass nigga workin for Uber won't stop a bullet from crashing against his head if that was what was supposed to happen. He could get his shit split by picking up the wrong mafucka. Or hell, the bullet ain't even gotta be for dawg. Shit, he could be crossing the street and a black Benz with a nigga named Cass sitting behind the wheel could hit him," he joked. "Death is inevitable, Ryann. No one is invincible."

"But you walk around like you are," I blurted out. "You do shit that makes people want to kill you."

He shrugged, "Because I don't give a fuck, sweetheart."

"If you don't give a fuck about what you dying will do to me, then you need to just take me back to the block and things will just have to go back to the way they were."

He was selfish.

I'd just told him everything that scared me about his lifestyle choices, but he sits there and tells me that he don't give a damn about living or dying.

"I didn't say I didn't care about the way it'd effect you, Ryann," he said. "But you can't let your fear stop this shit from happenin. I won't let it."

"Promise me this one thing—

"I don't like promises."

"Just listen," I yelled. He sighed I continued. "Promise me you won't get killed.. or something....promise me that I won't have to live without you."

He chuckled and looked away, "Yo, I can't do that—

"Stop laughing, Cass," I said looking down in embarrassment.

I knew I was asking him something silly, but I asked him anyway. My brothers had promised me that they would be as safe as possible, why couldn't Cass do that for me at least? I needed something to keep my sanity intact, even if just a little bit.

He grabbed the sides of my face, "I'm not laughing at you, Ryann. Look at me." I swallowed and looked into his eyes, then he said, "I'll do my best, aight?"

That's all I wanted to hear. I just wanted some kind of securement. I needed to know that he wouldn't be out here starting shit, looking for ways to get himself killed just because he didn't care.

"Okay."

"I need something from you," he paused. "I won't pressure you baby, but I need you to sort through yo shit. I don't share."

I nodded, "You won't have to."

*

I was sitting on the porch with Omni, Nek, and Ashlee when Cass's beamer pulled up at the trap across the street. Butterflies immediately filled the pit of my stomach. Shit was crazy, the affect he had on me and I hadn't even seen his face yet. Just knowing it was him sitting behind the wheel of the car excited me.

Last night was amazing. We didn't fuck or anything like that, but we just chilled in the car for hours, talking. I couldn't believe how easy talking to him came once I loosened up. He was a great conversationalist. I would have never guessed that.

But still, I didn't know much about him. It's crazy... the conversation flowed perfectly but we didn't talk about Cass. We talked about me and just everyday shit. There was still so much to learn about him. We'd spent hours together yesterday, but he didn't share much about himself with me. I knew of every detail on his face. I knew about the gap between his teeth, that he barely showed. I knew about the very small mole near his eyebrow. But about him? I knew nothing, outside of the fact that he was a drug dealer.

"I think I'm going to spend the night here, babe," said Omni, looking down at her phone shaking her head.

I snatched my attention away from the car across the street and said, "You know you're welcome anytime. What's goin on?"

She shrugged and pulled her bottom lip into her mouth, "I'm just tired of Juice ass."

"Trouble in paradise?" asked Ashlee with a smirk.

"No, no trouble. I just...I just need to be away for the night," Omni said before putting her Faygo Moon Mist pop up to her mouth.

"Like he can't just come over here," said Ashlee before sucking her teeth. "You better find you a nigga to crawl up under. Hell, who am I kidding? Juice will find your ass there too."

"She was talkin to Ryann, LeeLee," said Shaneka with a little giggle. "You stay fucking with that girl."

Shaneka was basically fully recovered. It was almost as if she didn't even get shot. My girl was back and in full effect, face beat to the gawds, rocking a body hugging sundress, pulling new niggas and all that. I was happy to have her back. She was the breath of fresh air that her shit talking sister wasn't. Surprisingly, her being home had calmed Ashlee down a lot. Ashlee spent the majority of her time taking care of Shaneka. Auntie had come down for about a week, but it was Ashlee who was a huge help to Nek.

"Ain't nobody stunting that miserable ass girl," I heard Omni say with a giggle.

In a matter of seconds, Cass had stolen my attention again. Right after I told Omni she could stay here, I was back to looking across the street. He had climbed out of his car and was approaching a group of four, but his eyes stayed on me. I smiled a little and he nodded at me.

I was happy as hell Dinero was still out driving people around. Uber had him hella busy since yesterday and I was perfectly fine with that. Perfect fucking timing, right? I couldn't wait to slide back onto the leather seats of Cass's beamer. I no longer gave a damn about how I was going to get away undetected with a block full of people. The moment I saw him pull up on the block, I stopped caring. I just wanted to be around him.

"Damn bitch, you eye fuckin' ain't you?" said Ashlee stepping in the way, blocking my view.

Omni giggled, "Uh huh, she sholl is. That bitch is in love, you hear me? She went to jail for that nigga."

"Bitch liked to do hard time for a whole ass stranger though. Where they do that aaaaat?" said Ashlee before she and Omni went into a fit of laughter.

"Waaaaait, how come I'm just hearing about this jail shit?" said Shaneka, scooting to the edge of her chair to get a better look at me. "You really fuck with that nigga, huh?"

I sucked my teeth, "Nek, they over exaggerated. I spent a couple hours in jail over a petty ass gun charge." I pointed between Ashlee and Omni, "Jokes. You bitches got jokes," I said with a slight chuckle.

"Jail is jail, and people don't go to jail for niggas they don't care about," said Shaneka before turning her cup up to her lips.

She had a point, but I had zero interest in having that conversation so I waved her off with a simple whatever.,

"Ohhh shit, he's coming over here girl," mumbled Omni. "D gone fuck you up."

I slightly moved Ashlee aside to get a quick glimpse of Cass coming across the street, "Give me some of your drink Lee."

Ashlee handed me her personal sized bottle of Hennessey, "Bitches don't need to cheat if they can't do it sober."

"You cheating on D with him? Oh God, girl didn't I tell you not to mess with him," said Shaneka rolling her eyes. "This shit is real."

I took a long swig of Ashlee's drink and began to finger comb my big wand curls. My heart began to pit patter against my chest and my mouth felt dry, even though I just had something to drink. It was Cass. It was always him. I reached down to the floor and picked up my bottle of Dole orange juice. While I had the bottle to my lips, Cass climbed the stairs.

"You ready?" he asked, without addressing anybody on the porch but me.

"Ummm, you really gone come up here without speaking," said Shaneka with a sly smirk.

Ashlee chimed in, "Right. Just as rude as they come."

He nodded at them and extended his hand out to me, which I happily grabbed hold of.

"Don't do anything I would do," said Ashlee with a hint of humor in her voice.

Her little sly remarks were straight up annoying me. Bitch thought it was cool to openly flirt with this nigga just because he talked reckless to her before. That nigga wasn't serious and she should know that by now. Thirsty bitch. With or without a whole ass boyfriend, I would smack her stupid ass in the mouth behind that cute shit she was popping off with towards Cass.

I looked over my shoulder at her, "Ashlee, shut ya dick suckers before I pop you in them, aight?"

She waved me off and sat back next to Omni who told me not to have too much fun. Shaneka sat there shaking her head at me while she sipped her drink. Shaneka was cool, but she had always been a little judgmental. I didn't give a damn about anybody judging me to be honest. Dinero and I were pretty much finished with at this point.

*

"Not now Dinero, please," I said as I held the front door to my house open.

It was around eight o'clock in the evening and I had just gotten back home from kicking it with Cass about thirty minutes ago. Dinero had called and called, but I ignored his call the entire time I was with Cass. I knew he would be calling me as soon as everybody on the block saw me get into Cass's car.

"I leave to go to work and you run off with that nigga," he yelled like he was crazy.

"Dawg, who are you yelling at? You trying to show off in front of ya bitch," I yelled back.

Standing across the street was Tiny, her squad, and a bunch of other people. Dinero was embarrassed and trying to seem like a man or some shit because any other time, he would not have yelled at me in front of the whole damn street. Ho nigga was taking advantage of none of my brothers being here. They didn't live here, but could show up at any given moment, especially if they were called over here because some shit was popping off.

But I didn't like to call them when it came to Dinero. They would beat him to death, do you hear me? He didn't know I was legit saving his stupid ass. He took advantage of my hesitation to call them too.

"You ain't gone tell me what was what?" he asked with a deep scowl on his face.

"We were talking about the fuckin' gun charge," I lied.

Yeah, so fucking what? I lied. I was sparing the niggas feelings and saving myself some argument. I was tired and just wanted to catch up on my shows. I could have told him the real, but that wasn't a conversation I wanted to have right now.

He ran his hand over his mouth, glanced over his shoulder at the crowd across the street and, nodded, "Oh, word? I heard it differently. Heard you are giddy as fuck, prancing around with another nigga making me look bad."

What the fuck was that little glance about?

"You sittin up discussing me with bitches, D? Is that what it is? Yo, on my life I'm about done with you, my nigga," I yelled, as I gripped the door with anger.

He glanced away and then back at me, "Fuck up out of here. She hit me off with some info, on the love."

I squinted my eyes at him and cocked my head a little, "Tiny?"

He chuckled and pinched his nose, "What do this have to—"

I got an instant attitude and a frown jumped right on my face, "Who told you something, Dinero? Tiny?" I paused. "Yeah that's who."

I nodded and walked away from the door. Slipping my Huaraches on, I decided I had about enough of this bitch clocking my every move. Type of bitch reports the every move of a bitch to their nigga? Where they do that at? She obviously wanted some attention, so I was about to straight give it to her.

"Man, where you about to go?" asked Dinero, easing his way into my house with a smirk. "You kill me getting mad at other people when you're in the wrong."

I shoved him so hard he went stumbling back onto the porch, "Fuck up outta hea, my nigga."

I was hot. As hot as I was right now, I was liable to punch him dead in his face. Stupid weak ass nigga. I didn't realize how much of a fuckin' weak piece of shit he was until we got together. When we were friends, he was the coolest. I loved being around him, but now? I hated the sight of him almost as much as I hated the sight of his apartment. He disgusted me. He's whack as fuck. Type of nigga was he? Straight up letting some female hit him up every single time I did something. He was feeding into it. Giving her what she wanted, when he should have curved her and put her in her place the first time she mentioned me. But nah, obviously Dinero didn't move like that. He moved the same way bitches moved.

"Yo, chill—"

I pushed the storm door open and it hit the house. Thankfully, not hard enough to shatter the glass—again.

"No, you chill. Comin' around here checking me and shit because of what a bitch said."

"What's going on?" asked Shonny, walking across the street with none other than Tiny herself.

My nostrils flared and I damn near fell down the stairs, I ran down them so fast. Shonny drew back and her hand went up to her mouth at the sight of the scars on my face.

"Ry, who did that? Did Dinero hit you?" she asked.

It had been weeks since I fell. I was treating the scars with Neosporin, but since I usually kept makeup on my face, no one had really seen them. They were healing, but they still looked a little bad.

"Is that nigga dead, bitch? Fuck you mean," I spat before transferring my rage to Tiny. "Fucks the deal, Tiny? You some type of private investigator now? You reporting my every move to this nigga?"

"What? I didn't tell him nothing. Bitch you betta—"

That bitch word always set me off. I drew my arm back and punched her in her face. She stumbled back and touched her bleeding nose.

At this point, everybody in the hood had ran down the street to my house to see what was going on. Tiny wouldn't square up with me though. She kept circling Shonny, talking shit. She was going on and on about how she hadn't told Dinero shit. I didn't believe that though, but since she wouldn't throw hands, I walked away. It would have been weak as hell of me to keep beating on her and she didn't want to fight. That's bully shit and I'm no bully.

"Ryann let me talk to you—

"Dinero, get the fuck away from my house," I yelled at the top of my lungs.

He held his hands up and backed away, "Aight, aight. You need some time..."

I sucked my teeth and dramatically sighed, hella annoyed, "No bitch, I need you to leave me alone. Period."

I walked into the house and slammed the door so hard, pictures on the wall fell.

*

"Boo-Baby... Boo-baby."

I woke up to Dinero siting on side of my bed and I'd like to fucking died. I didn't know what time it was, but it was pitch black in my room with the exception of the moonlight peeking through my window, shining on him.

"Dinero, how did you get in my house?" I asked sleepily as I turned over to grab my phone from the nightstand.

"Nek let me in," he said as he began to rub my feet.

I snatched them away and sat up against the headboard.

Nek has been getting on my mothafuckin' nerves. Bitch was too worried about what happened in my relationship. She's been so judgy, yet she's running around the hood getting trains ran on her and shit, but I've said nothing because at the end of the day, it's her life to fuck up—not mine.

I was too pissed because before I went to bed, I specifically told both Nek and LeeLee not to let Dinero in when he came over. I knew he'd be back. The shit that went down earlier was too much for him not to try to come diffuse the situation.

"I told you, I didn't want to see you," I said as I stole a quick glance at my .380 sitting on the nightstand to make sure it was still there. I wish I could grab that bitch without causing more issues.

"I know, Ry baby, but I love you too much to just let this shit go," he said shaking his head as he scooted close to the head of the bed.

I drew back when the heavy scent of liquor hit my nose. Dinero was drunk as hell and I wanted my gun now more than I did before. Niggas are emotional as hell when their drunk and I straight embarrassed Dinero earlier.

"D, you're drunk. Go home and sleep that shit off. We'll talk tomorrow—"

He jumped up from the bed and yelled, "No, we won't. Stop playing with me like I don't know how you operate, Ryann!"

I quickly grabbed my gun and stood up, "Go home or I swear to God—"

"You swear to God what? That you gon shoot me? Just because I love yo heartless ass? Damn boo-babyyyyy... why you doin' me like this?" he yelled with his chest heavily heaving up and down.

Dinero was crying. A grown as man was pacing my bedroom floor, crying real ass tears because I wanted to break up with him. How am I going to deal with this shit? This nigga is not a regular nigga. All this pussy out here and he's hella bent on me.

I leaned over and flicked the light to my lamp on, "I just want you to let it go. Let us go."

He staggered from side to side before quickly snatching my gun from my hands. I jumped back and held my trembling hands up. But he didn't point it at me, he pointed it at his temple.

"Fuck livin if I can't have my boo-baby," he said, heavily slurring over his words.

"Nek! LeeLee! Somebody please... please come help me," I cried.

I couldn't be around any shit like this. Dinero was tripping the fuck out. And for what, man? Our relationship was mediocrity at its best. Why was he reacting so emotionally? I just couldn't understand why he wouldn't just let me go. I couldn't break up with him and the shit was killing me.

Seconds later, LeeLee and Nek barged into the room. When they saw Dinero standing there with my gun to his head, their hands went up over their mouths and they gasped.

Nek was the only one to walk further into the room, "D... Please put the gun down."

"Tell me you won't leave me, Ryann," he said with tears pouring from his eyes. He didn't care that he was straight embarrassing himself in front of Ashlee and Shaneka either.

My bottom lip trembled as I said, "I won't leave you, D."

How was I going to get myself out of this situation without killing him in the process?

- Cass -

I got, I got, I got, I got
Loyalty, got royalty inside my DNA
Cocaine quarter piece, got war and peace inside my
DNA
I got power, poison, pain and joy inside my DNA
I got hustle though, ambition, flow, inside my DNA
I was born like this, since one like this
Immaculate conception
I transform like this, perform like this
Was Yeshua's new weapon
I don't contemplate, I meditate, then off your
fucking head
This that put-the-kids-to-bed

I glanced at the time on the dash, and it was just after nine-thirty in the morning. I was blasting Kendrick Lamar's DNA, pushing the whip through the hood about to link with one of my young dawgs. Linking with my nigga Chicago was always the first thing I did in the morning. He gave me word on the light work, whereas Luck kept me laced with all of the important shit. I liked to link with him in the hood because either before or after, I would hit Delux Coney Island for some breakfast.

I wiped sleep from the corner of my eye, as I pulled up behind his Hummer. He was standing outside, leaning against his truck, chiefing on a blunt. I shifted the car in park, grabbed my bottle water, and hopped out.

For it to be so early in the morning, it was hot as shit. Swear a nigga needed to invest in some sunscreen or some shit. The sun was mad vicious, beaming directly over me. I adjusted my jean shorts and treaded up to him.

"What up, G," said Chicago slapping hands with me.

"What's good?" I asked as I twisted the cap off the bottle of water. "What's the word?"

"Keys BM," he blew out a gust of air. "She came down to the trap early, early this morning crying."

I took a swig of my water then asked, "'Bout what?"

"Say the kids hungry."

We were posted up on Maine St., chopping it up like we did every morning. I cocked my head to the side a little, watching the flowers across the street sway in the hot breeze that had swept by. As I stared across the street, I thought about how it felt to be hungry. I used to starve. So much to a point that I use to eat the roaches crawling around my crib. I was so thirsty that I use to run out to the backyard and drink the rain water that this dirty ass bucket use to collect. Being hungry almost killed me.

My top lip twitched, thinking about everything I've gone through. You think the starving stopped once I was placed in the system? Shit no. It did, momentarily, for the short period of time I was with Ms. Mable and Mr. Gregory. But the moment I left them, I was starved, even living in a house full of food. Everybody ate, but me.

Leaning against the truck, I extended my hand out to Chicago for the blunt. He gave it to me and I took three pulls from it before handing it back.

I then fished around the pockets of my shorts until I retrieved a small knot of money. I then handed him a G and said, "Go grab them some food. Stock 'em up with some shit. Hit Sam's Club, Walmart, all dem shits. Grab diapers and household necessities too. Don't hit her off with any cash, though."

I didn't know Keys baby mom's from a can of paint, so I didn't know what kind of shit she could be on. But what I wouldn't sit back and allow were kids to go hungry. So, yeah, I'll stock the crib up, but putting cash in a broad's hands? Nah, not happenin.

"You sho? Man, that's that niggas responsibility, G," said Chicago, shaking his head in dismay.

"The fuck I look like letting kids go hungry? Feed 'em," I snapped.

Being reminded of my fucked up childhood always put me in a bad headspace. And the fact that this stupid fuck thought those kids should suffer because I'm not their pops pissed me off on another level.

He nodded and quickly switched the subject, sensing that I didn't want to talk shit else about it.

"Word is, Maino and Rome didn't give Mitch that bad batch." He kicked at a can rolling down the street and said, "One of the crack head bitches he fucked with said one of the young niggas who usually sold him dope burnt off right before his body was found."

I fished my small comb from my back pocket and began to comb my beard, "Oh, tru shit, uh? One of our niggas? What else auntie say?"

He nodded his head, "Uh huh... same thing that nigga was sayin... that the FEDS are closer than we think, said we had a snake in our camp."

A sudden flash of light snatched my attention from Chicago and I quickly sent my eyes in the direction it came from. I squinted and could see someone crouching down behind the sunflowers across the street. How close did she mean?

"Yo, you seen that," I asked Chicago as I pushed myself up off the truck and stuffed my comb back in my pocket.

"Saw what?" he asked, following behind me.

My attention was on the movement behind the sunflowers. I could hear Chicago steady asking me if I wanted him to squeeze off, but I was too focused to respond to him. I made it across the street just as the sound of twigs breaking underneath someone's fast feet sounded as they ran through the garden, trying to get away from me. Fuckin' FEDs. I knew they would come back eventually. I just wanted to catch the fuck nigga. That's all I wanted to do. Rough 'eem up, possibly smack the piss out a nigga for invading my privacy or somethin'. But after just hitting some fire green, my smoker lungs wasn't about shit and I couldn't catch up to them.

Chicago finally caught up with me, trying to catch his breath, "What it is, G? You want me to keep after the nigga?"

I ran my tongue over my bottom lip, shaking my head no, "I'ma catch 'eem. On mafuckin' life I am."

"You aight, my nigga," asked Chicago standing in front of me with a frown on his face. "1-8-7 written all ova ya' mug."

I scratched the back of my neck and turned to head back to my whip. Nah, I wasn't aight. I needed to get these fuck ass FEDs up off me. I needed to find out what it was they had on me. Ain't no crime against kicking back, minding yo own fuckin' business. So what's with the pictures? Last time, I was at the crib in a robe chilling. Now, I'm just chopping it up with my guy. What kind of evidence is there in chilling? I needed to link with Scotty ASAP. I needed to find out what was what before I lost my cool.

"You up, my nigga?" asked Chicago.

I nodded and climbed in my whip, turned the key and burnt off. I needed to stay out of the way until I found out what it was they were trying to put on me.

*

"You can't tell me shit else, Scot," I asked Scotty as I sat behind the wheel of my car watching her from afar.

Scotty sighed, "Nah man. You know that stuff is confidential. I'll try to find out as much as I can."

"You do that and hit me up the moment you do," I said before hanging up on him and cranking the engine up.

I shifted the car in drive and pulled over to the curb where Ryann and her girls were walking from the gas station. She looked over at the unfamiliar truck with tints, rolled her eyes and went back to walking with her girls. I tapped on the horn a couple times, just to annoy her mean ass. She looked again and frowned.

I rolled the window down just enough to hear what was being said. The wild one I talked shit to that day... Ashlee, she yelled out hey and I said nothing. Another one of the girls sucked her teeth and said, "Lee you always trying to jump on the ballers before anybody else."

Ryann kept walking, talking to Juice's girl, paying me no mind. This is why I fucked with her. She wasn't moved by shit like niggas pushing fly whips. Those other two broads were ready to let a nigga smash and they haven't even seen my mug. Loose bitches.

"Ayo shorty in the ugly ass slides," I called out.

Ryann whipped her head in my direction fast as hell and a smile spread wide as hell.

"They can't be too ugly; Rih making a killing off of them," she said after turning back around, steady walking.

"Who is that?" said Ashlee to Ryann.

"I don't know. Some thirsty nigga," she replied like she really didn't know who I was.

I pulled up a little further down the block and shifted the car in park. I hopped out and the three girls Ryann were walking with all sucked their teeth at the same time.

I licked my lips and walked alongside Ryann with my hands stuffed in my pockets.

"What's ya name, sweetheart?" I asked, playing along with her game.

"Anonymous," she shot back, trying her damnedest to keep that gorgeous ass smile off her face.

I draped my arm over her shoulder, looked over my shoulder at her girls, and said, "Y'all mind if I kidnap Anonymous? Shorty need a new pair of slides."

Ashlee rolled her eyes up and said, "Y'all being corny, but the whole hood watching, and everybody know this bitch gotta whole nigga."

"Fuck 'em," I said. "You feel me, Anonymous, baby?"

Ryann's arm was covered in goosebumps, and her cheeks were rosy red. This little game she was playing was short lived. As soon as my skin touched hers, it was over. Only I had this effect on her. Not her nigga, and damn sho not a stranger trying to get on.

"Y'all gone cover for me," she asked her girls.

"Ryann..." said one of the girls I barely seen around here.

Ryann sucked her teeth, "You know what? I don't give a fuck either way."

*

"Cass, how much are those? On some real shit, all I need are some Nike slides," said Ryann, trying to grab the Givenchy slides from my hands.

I turned away from her, "Fuck on, lil' mama. I got it. Feet that pretty only deserve to be covered in the best."

As soon as we left the hood, I headed straight for Somerset. I had some business to tend to, but I took care of business all day, every day. Fucks the point of making all of this money if I couldn't spend it? I didn't get to do this. I couldn't remember the last time I been at the mall. All a nigga ever had time to do was hit Footlocker or Villa for some quick shit.

Ryann popped her lips and said, "I meeeeean, you do have a point there. These mafuckas are about as fine as I am."

I laughed and we continued to the counter where I sat her slides and a few things for me down on. We had just gotten here and went straight to Neiman's. She thought I was talking shit about getting her some new slides, but I was dead ass.

"You know her?" asked Ryann, nodding to the back of the store with a mean mug.

I looked over my shoulder and fished around my pockets for money, "A lil bit."

She sucked her teeth, "What you mean a lil? Bitch looking over here like y'all are a lot more than a lil acquainted."

I stood in front of her and grabbed her waist, "Who am I here with? Fuck you acting jealous for?"

Ryann drew back, "Jealous? Not even. I just don't like the shit."

Ryann's boyfriend didn't exist when we were together. When we were together, we were *together*, and we treated the shit as such. She was territorial as fuck when it came to me and vice versa. Shit killed me when I had to leave her, just for her to go back to her nigga though. But when we were kicking it like this? That pussy nigga didn't exist. Shorty even had the nigga on **DO NOT DISTURB**.

"Hey Cass," said Genie standing in line behind us.

I nodded and handed a stack to the cashier with one arm steady wrapped around Ryann.

"You can' t talk—

"Nah bitch, not while he's with me. You keep trying that cute shit, you won't be talking either," said Ryann, cutting Genie off. "Dead ass will be picking ya raggedy teeth up off the floor."

I pressed my mouth close to her ear, "What I tell you about that nut shit? Queens don't move like that."

Ryann sighed and her nostrils flared while she nodded.

Genie sucked her teeth, "Damn Cass... she got you like that, huh?"

"Stop talkin," I said to her, with my eyes still locked in on Ryann's.

"What—"

"Bitch, he said stop talkin. This nigga is trying to save ya life," said Ryann.

Genie sucked her teeth, "Tuh—"

I finally snatched my eyes away from Ryann's to lock eyes with Genie. She knew I didn't tolerate any type of disrespect. I didn't partake in any of this petty shit. Bitch only spoke because I was out with someone who wasn't her. She was jealous because all I did was stick dick to her. Spending five hundred on some slides for Genie? Never. The only thing I ever fed the bitch was dick. She wasn't treated like this and I fucked with her for months, meanwhile I just met Ryann, and baby could have whatever she liked.

Instead of saying another word, Genie sat her things on the counter and walked out of the store.

I wrapped both my arms around Ryann and kissed her on the forehead, "Crazy mafucka."

"Crazy about you."

- Ryann -

*Remorse: deep regret or guilt for a wrong
committed*

"Don't let go," said Cass, looking at me over his shoulder.

"I won't," I replied with my arms wrapped tightly around his body.

I was on the back of Cass's Ducati, getting ready to go for a ride. I had never been on the back of a motorcycle and had I been with anyone else, I would have been scared shitless. But I was with Cass. With him, I felt my safest. With him, I didn't feel the need to have my .380 tucked in my waistband. With him, I felt like I didn't need anything or anybody else.

He cranked the engine up and I rested my feet on the foot pegs.

"You ready?" he asked, with a voice slightly muffled by his helmet.

I told him I was and held onto him tighter. He then took off and I laid my head on his back.

Since we had been kicking it so much, spending time with him had become easier and easier. The remorse I thought I would feel behind sneaking around with him had subsided. Remorse only sat in when I left him to be with Dinero. As fucked up as it may sound, I felt like this is where I was supposed to be.

Cass had been so patient, but he made sure to always remind me that time was of the essence. I knew this. I was well aware of all of the time I was wasting with Dinero. Actually, I wasn't wasting time with his dumb ass because I barely saw him these days. After that nigga put my gun to his head, I've been kind of straight on him. I haven't broken up with him because that shit scared me. He did come over the next day saying how he was drunk last night and couldn't remember anything. When I told him what he did, he told me he was tripping and that he apologized. Since then, we didn't talk about it, but it still haunted me, and I was still afraid to break up with him.

The night air beat against my skin, as I felt like I was soaring. Cass had to be doing about eighty on this freeway. Instead of fear, I felt so alive. Like I hadn't truly been living up until this very moment.

I reached for my camera dangling on my neck and he yelled, "No pictures, Ryann."

I nodded and placed my hand back around his waist. I was supposed to be home hours ago. I was supposed to check in with Dinero right after I left my last photography gig for the day. But I didn't. I just didn't have a single fuck to give.

As soon as I left the reception hall, I met Cass at American Coney Island on W. Lafayette not too far from where the wedding reception was. Dinero hadn't crossed my mind once. I was too wrapped up falling in love with someone else. Too wrapped up in the thrill of being with Cass.

He took the exit off the freeway and began to slow up. He then stopped at a red light and asked me why I hadn't tapped him like he told me to if he was driving too fast. I told him he was driving at the perfect speed.

He lifted the mask off his helmet and looked over his shoulder at me, "You like that crazy shit, huh? Trying to take pictures and shit while I'm floating this mafucka."

"Yes," I replied with a broad smile and a slight giggle. Then I whispered in his ear, "Push it to a hundred."

"Shit no. I'm riding with precious cargo, baby. If I was by my lonely. But with you? Never."

He then put his mask back over his face and took off.

He always talked about how I was so precious. Cass treated me like I was perfect, despite my flaws. Despite the way I did my boyfriend. Every time I asked him if he thought I was shady and disloyal because of the way I carelessly cheated on Dinero, he'd tell me no. And then, when I'd ask if he questioned my loyalty because of it, he told me no. I couldn't decipher why. But then he made it perfectly clear to me. Cass said we met a little too late in life. Had he shown up in time, Dinero wouldn't even be in the equation. He called it a flaw in the universe. Now, we were fixing that flaw. And because of my fear, it was taking a little longer than he liked. He didn't like it, but he didn't push me either.

Fifteen minutes later, we were pulling up at the gate that lead into his community. I was already familiar with this spot. I'd finessed my way in this bitch not too long ago. Thank God for the helmet I wore, because I'm sure the security guard would have remembered my pitiful ass.

It had been a minute since I've had to snap pictures of him from afar, though. The last time I snuck a picture of him, he almost caught me again, so I said fuck it. These days I did it when we were together, in the open. Cass hated to be photographed. He said taking pictures made him feel awkward, but did he not know how incredible he photographed? He had to be unaware of the regal features he possessed. I'd sneak a picture of him here and there. Then there were the times when he knew I was takin pictures of him. All he did was ruin the shit by posing too hard or being too uncomfortable. I was thankful for the collection I had of him already.

Cass pulled into his driveway and we both hopped off the bike. I handed him the helmet I wore, and he snapped it onto the bike. He held his freehand out for me to grab before we headed up to the house. There was that spark again. Every time we were together, at least once during our stay together, we'd shock each other.

He unlocked the door and stood back so that I could walk inside. This was my first time here. We spent a lot of time out on dates and just kicking it in his car, but never alone like this. I wondered what tonight would bring? Would I really cheat on my boyfriend? Was I turning into the very thing I despised?

Cass flicked a light on, and my eyes widened in surprise. Now this is how a mothafucka lives, okay? That shit Dinero is on? Nah. Cass's home was spotless, and looked as if he had an interior designer come out. The hardwood floors were spotless. So spotless, I slipped my shoes off at the front door. He laughed and told me I didn't have to. I told him I felt like I needed to. Stepping further into the house, I took in the rest of the home, impressed. He had a cream-colored sectional, and a glass coffee table sitting in the middle of the floor, on top of a plush, brown rug. It was so simple, yet so nice.

*

Cass was showing me how to break my gun down, but I wasn't listening to a single word that left his lips. I had my eyes on them, but I couldn't make out shit he was saying. I was too busy trying to stop myself from kissing him. My lips would be their most comfortable upon his. They always were.

"Ryann," he said.

I stopped biting my bottom lip and looked up at him with raised eyebrows, "Huh?"

He sat the broken-down gun on the coffee table and licked his lips before grabbing my chin. He tilted my head back and kissed me on my lips. They were as soft as they looked… just as soft as I always. When he pulled away, I sat there with my lips steady puckered and my eyes closed, like how those goofy bitches in the movies do. I felt silly as hell when I opened them just to discover he had gone back to working on the gun.

I annoyingly rolled my eyes, "Cass, I'm not trying to hear about no damn gun."

"You're not trying to fuck neither," he blatantly said. "Soon as I get ready to stick dick to you, you gone freeze up like you do all of the time, sweetheart."

I swallowed and looked away. I did freeze up every time things got a little too steamy. Cass thought it was because of Dinero. That was only part of the reason. The other part was that, if I gave myself to him, infatuation would certainly turn into addiction. Cass would go from a serious crush to someone I truly could not live without. Fucking him would take my vulnerability to another level. Fucking him would mean I was truly cheating on Dinero. Wasn't that what I was already doing though? Still…sex…it would make it real.

I scooted closer to him and took the gun from his hand. I then straddled him and cupped his face in my hands.

"You have a perfect face, Cass," I honestly told him.

He looked away and told me to gone on somewhere with that shit, like he always did when I told him he had a perfect face. He didn't believe it. He talked that cocky shit all of the time, but I knew he wasn't as confident as he led on to believe. I didn't care if he didn't believe what I said—I meant it.

I kissed his forehead, "Perfectly shaped forehead." I then kissed the sides of his face, "Perfect bone structure." Then my lips landed on the tip of his wide, fat nose, "Perfect nose." I then licked my lips and ran my thumb over his full, soft, succulent lips, "And these lips..." I shook my head, leaned forward and kissed him on his lips. This time, I parted them with my tongue, and let it creep inside.

Cass never tongue kissed me. And when our tongues finally did the tango, I found out why. He didn't know how to French kiss. I was his first tongue kiss. Grabbing the sides of his face, I twirled it inside of his mouth, and he eventually matched my rhythm. I then sucked his thick bottom lip, and he followed suite by sucking my top lip.

I could feel his dick grow hard though his shorts, and my breath got caught up someplace in the back of my throat.

He pulled away and said, "Breath."

I exhaled, and then inhaled. Pulling my lips into my mouth, I looked away in embarrassment. We were at a point in our 'situationship' where he knew things about me. He knew how he made me feel, and sometimes I just forgot to fuckin breathe. How crazy is that? Cass literally took my breath away.

He lowered his head and I ran my hands over his dreadlocks. Snaking my hands around the back of his head, I undid his hair tie. He grabbed my wrist, stopping me from letting his dreads hand freely, but I carried on anyhow. He eventually let me have my way, as he always does when I go to let his hair hang over his broad shoulders.

I ran my fingers through his messy locs as a moan escaped my lips. He had his mouth covering the top of my right breast, twiddling my nipple. *Breathe, bitch, breathe,* I reminded myself not wanting him to witness me breathless anymore. That made me feel weak. Was it that Cass made me weak? Oh, yes, he made me weak beyond understanding.

He lowered my spaghetti strap over my arms, and then he lowered my shirt over my breast. He ran his thick tongue over his bottom lip when my breast feel freely. *Don't stop him, bitch. Don't freeze up. Breathe, baby, breathe.* It was always at this point that I lost all control.

His mouth covered my protruding nipple and I let out a soft moan, feeling bolts of electricity radiate through my entire being. My fingertips, and the tip of toes tingled. I quivered and Cass wrapped his arms around my body, holding me so close to him that I could feel his heart beating against my chest. It was racing. Almost as fast as mine. Or was it faster? He wanted this just a bad as I did, and I wanted to give it to him. I needed to give it to him. I never wanted to do anything as bad as I wanted to give my body to him.

He pulled his mouth away from my nipple, and whispered in my ear, "I got you."

He had me. I know this. On several occasions, Cass had me. When no one else did. When the weight of the world got just a little too heavy, I could always rely on conversation or just a photo of him to calm me. When anxiety got the best of me, I'd close my eyes and envision his perfect imperfections and everything would then be right in the world. So those three words—I got you—spilling from those dark, wet lips of his had meaning to them. I believed him.

I nodded and he stood up from the couch with my legs wrapped around his waist. He then carried me to another part of the house. A part of the house I'd later refer to as The place where magic happened. He pushed the towering double doors open and carried me into the dark room. With the flick of a switch, the room was brightly illuminated. I climbed down from his waist and looked up at him with lustful eyes.

But what sat behind his eyes was something hard to pinpoint. Imagine looking for one of your most prized possessions. You've looked for it for days, weeks even. And then suddenly, out of the clear blue while minding your business you find it. Imagine the look on your face. The satisfaction. The pleasure. The relief. The look of finding it. Cass looked at me like that. And not just now. Every time our eyes met, he looked at me like he found *it*. His eyes said more than his mouth ever said.

While staring into those dark irises of his, I lowered my leggings. We've never gotten this far. The moment his mouth touched the skin of my body, I'd lose the air in my lungs. I would freeze up. But not tonight. Tonight, I found my air. Tonight, in losing control, I found it as well.

Cass's eyes left mine, and traveled every curve on my body. He then grabbed my hips and pulled me close to his body, where his dick poked at my stomach. I grabbed the elastic band of his shorts, and eagerly pulled them down. I gripped his dick, and looked down at it. I gasped at the sight of how long and thick it was. And good God it was dark. So dark, almost three shades darker than his already dark skin.

I looked up at him with questioning eyes, wondering, how in the fuck he was going to fit that inside of me? It wasn't straight like I was used to. It was curved to the left. Dinero... he was average, at around six inches, and not as thick. I've never had anything like what Cass was working with.

"Breathe," he said.

Fuck. It had happened again.

"You sure you ready, sweetheart? If you're not—

I quickly dropped down to my knees, and covered his dick with my mouth, cutting him off midsentence. I was ready. Or at least I thought I was. The moment his dick hit my tonsils, Dinero crossed my mind. I was cheating. I couldn't cheat on him anymore. I had to leave him. I had no other choice but to. I was at a point now that I didn't give a solid fuck about ruining our friendship, or him threatening to end his life. I didn't give a got damn about what people were going to say. I had my Cass. My sweetest obsession. Nothing else mattered.

Cass backed up against the wall, and began to pant heavily. I gripped the base of his dick and slowly slid his dick down my throat. He exhaled, and relaxed against the wall while I covered his dick with saliva. I didn't realize just how turned on I was until I felt an orgasm wash over me. I moaned, and my eyebrows snapped together as my body went into light convulsions. Looking up at Cass, I could see that he was just as turned on by this as I was. A light moan escaped his lips and my pussy pulsated at the sweet melody to my ears.

He began to pant heavily, while biting on his bottom lip. He wore a frown of pure pleasure on his face, while he ran his fingers through my hair. I could tell that he wanted to pull it, but held back out of respect. But I wanted sex in the most disrespectful way possible. I grabbed his wrist, encouraging the roughness. He had no problem obliging as he began to vigorously fuck my face. I gagged on his dick, having to adjust to the size of new dick hitting my tonsils. I don't think Dinero ever got so far down my throat. His dick wouldn't allow it.

Without warning, Cass grabbed a handful of my hair and pulled me away from his dick.

"Bend over," he demanded.

"But I—

He snatched me up to my feet and pushed me onto the bed, where I was then penned up against the headboard, on my knees. Cass then proceeded to roughly pull my thong down. He pressed his body against me, his dick poking at my bare ass cheeks. I moaned and he grabbed a handful of my hair, yanking my head to the opposite side.

"Tell me you want it," he whispered in my ear.

"I want it. I need it," I said, damn near in tears.

Cass had no idea. He was very unaware of just how much my pussy craved this very moment. I wanted him to touch it. I wanted him to treat my pussy in ways she's never been treated before. I wanted his massive dick buried so deep into my walls, that I was literally rendered speechless. I wanted his dick all over me. Inside of my pussy, in the forbiddance of my asshole, on my face—everywhere.

He let my hair go, and backed away. I arched my back completely down, anticipating the feel of his dick filling me up. But what came next was a surprise. I felt his thick, wet tongue slide over my wetness. My knees buckled and I gripped the side of the headboard for added leverage. Cass grabbed both my ass cheeks and spread them apart, lapping over my pussy like it was the best thing he'd ever tasted. He moaned into my pussy, and my eyes rolled to the back of my head. I had never had head so fucking good in my entire life.

After devouring my pussy for all of ten minutes, I had lost count of how many times I came.

He reached over to the nightstand, where he pulled the top drawer open, fishing around for a condom I assumed. After retrieving a condom, he tore into it with his teeth, and then skillfully slid it over his dick. Within seconds, I felt the tip of it poking at my small hole. I grabbed hold of one of the pillows, as he slowly entered me inch by inch. I was so wet, but he was so thick that it was a struggle to get inside.

Cass pushed my back down a little, and began to go further inside. I bit on my bottom lip, and tightly closed my eyes shut as he began to move into me in a rhythmic fashion. He rubbed the dip in my back and I shuddered. When I felt him enter me completely, I flinched and groaned.

He leaned forward and whisper in my ear, "I got you. Relax. Let me take care of you."

His voice was like sweet music to my ears, the huskiness of it, the low whisper... it was all just so got damn sexy.

I nodded and he grabbed my hips, fucking me at a slow pace, almost as if he was really taking care of me. Pampering my pussy with delicacy. So slow, but steady at the same time. So passionate. So damn good. His dick reached places that had yet to be explored. He was so deep inside of me, hitting my most sensitive spots. Making me crazier than I already was. His rough, rough hands around my waist, gripping me in a fashion that said he didn't want me to go anywhere. He wanted me just where he had me. Bent over on his bed, back arched, under his control, with his dick buried deep within my sugary walls. He held me in a way that said that he'd wanted me here for so long.

Cass's hands went from gripping my waist to grabbing my ass cheeks, where he held them open, getting more access to my pussy. How much more did he want? He was already deep inside of me. So deep that I felt like he was making love to my fuckin' ovaries. So deep that there were tears trickling down my cheeks. Passionate tears, laced with addiction. He was a drug I knew I would want all of the time. A drug I wouldn't mind overdosing on. I was getting it yet I was already feigning for it. Dreading the seconds, minutes, and hours I would be forced to be without it. Cass's dick was so fucking good that I wanted to detach it from his body and carry it in my purse. I wanted to hold it captive. I didn't want another bitches pussy on it. Hell, I didn't even want them to think about it.

"Oh God," I moaned, as he gravitated his hips in a circular motion, stirring all inside of my creamy goodness. "Fuhhh...Fuck me," I breathed out, wanting him to beat my pussy the fuck up.

I threw my hips back on him, and my pussy gushed.

He mumbled, "Damn." And then went back to gripping my hips.

Without warning, he picked me up, stood up off the bed, and slammed me up and down on his dick, from the back. My titties bounced all over the place, and I did nothing to control them. I couldn't, for I was under Cass's control. He grabbed my thighs, and bent my legs back as he continued to pound inside of me. I was in reverse cowgirl, except I was in the fucking air.

"Tell me," he said as he continued to mercilessly fuck me crazy.

"Tell you...tell you what."

He then slickly slipped a finger in my sopping wet asshole, and bit my earlobe, "That it's mine. I own this." He quickly twirled me around so that I was facing him. "Tell me."

"It's yours," I yelled, as I wrapped my legs and arms around him.

He grunted, "Mmm... Cassim owns this mafucka. Say it."

He looked like a crazed animal, with his mouth was lazily ajar, and his dipped eyebrows, lightly coated with perspiration.

"Cass own's—

He roughly slapped me on the ass, "Cassim."

I screamed out, "Cassim...Cassim.. oh God...Cassim owns this mothafucka! Yes the fuck he do!"

I was just as crazy as he was. I viciously bit down on my bottom lip as I felt yet another orgasm coming on. I ran my tongue over my bottom lip, tasting the bitterness of blood. I'd bitten myself so hard that I drew blood. Pain was overpowered by pleasure, as cum began to run down my thighs. I buried my face in his neck as he continued to bless me with his heavenly dick. Good God it was so good. I was crying real ass tears as he slowed his pace, and planted the most softest kisses ever on my neck. He 'd gone from fucking me like a wild man, to making love to me almost as sensual as he did when he first entered me.

There was so much passion behind every stroke that it sent tingles all over my body. He tensed up a bit, and quickened his pace. He went from kissing my neck, to biting and sucking. Sucking and biting which I did not protest upon. I let him. I let him nibble on my skin as he grunted and moaned through his own orgasm.

I'd finally had some of Cass—no, not Cassim. His government name even sounded like some African king type shit.

Panting heavily, after his orgasm, steady deep within me he said, "Don't give that weak ass nigga anymore of my pussy."

I was too drained to reply, and lazily laid there.

He smacked me on the ass, "You heard me?"

"Yes," I quickly replied. "I won't."

I meant it. I would never play myself again by allowing Dinero to slide into me with that mediocre dick of his.

*

I woke up to the sound of my phone ringing. It took me a minute to realize where I was, until I looked across the room. Cassim sat in a chair, with my camera in his hands. Fear washed over me as I silenced the ringer and asked him what he was doing with my camera.

He pushed himself up from his chair and treaded over to me with a scowl on his face.

"You a fuckin' FED," he yelled so loudly that the bass from his voice sent vibrations through my body. "You come around, finessin' the fuck out a nigga. As a matta of fact," he roughly scratched at his head and said, "You straight pretended not to even know a nigga. But shit, in this camera is pictures of me before I even stepped to you. Hundreds. You want to explain what is what before I split cha fuckin' wig? At least give me that!"

I was frozen. I didn't know what to do. His yelling, his anger...after a night like last night... it snatched my voice away. Took every bit of feistiness, and hoodness right up out of my ass. How would I explain this? How could I? The recent pictures, I could explain. The old, ancient ones? And oh God...the ones of him standing on his balcony? How... How could I explain?

He didn't give me a chance to.

He dove onto the bed, and wrapped his hands around my neck. I didn't put up a fight. I didn't try to scream. I didn't claw at his hands. I let him squeeze. I let him choke me. Not because I wanted to die because death petrified me to the point of paralysis. In this moment, I knew that death was inevitable. I didn't have my gun. Cassim was ten times my size, and a raging bull. Fighting would only make it worst. So, I let him. I let him choke me until he took it upon himself to let me go.

"Fuck," He yelled, as he paced the bedroom floor, obviously battling between killing me and not killing me. Or maybe he wanted me to suffer? Yea, Cassim was so mad that simply choking me wouldn't suffice. He had that evil, animalistic, rip a person a part type of anger.

He scratched the tip of his nose, and I'd like to died when he threw my camera across the room. It hit the wall so hard, that it shattered. Watching the pieces fly was symbolic to the way my heart was breaking. Damn the thousand dollar camera. I knew that from this day forward, Cassim wouldn't trust me.

My eyes averted to the memory card sitting on top of the rubbish, and his did too. It was like he read my mind, because seconds later, he snatched it up and stuffed it into the pocket of his basketball shorts.

"I'm not—I'm not a FED," I managed to get out in the middle of a whimper.

I felt like a small child. Defenseless, scared, and just weak.

He slowly approached me, with his chest rapidly rising and falling. Again, he wrapped his hands around my neck. This time, he lifted me from the bed, and I dangled in the air. He was going to kill me. I searched his eyes for just a hint of who he was last night. The love, the passion... but he was gone. Last night, he introduced me to Cassim. This morning, I was facing Cass.

"You were at my fuckin' house...In my fuckin'....In my mothafucka backyard. Bitch, don't insult me like I didn't see the picture," he yelled.

He then looked away, and again, let go of my neck. I went crashing onto the bed.

"Cassim...I swear to God," I said through a hoarse voice, with tears now pouring down my face. "I'm—I'm not."

Had it been anyone else who'd put their hands on me, I would have found something to kill him with. But it was my Cassim. The man I simply adored. And he was confused, and he was upset. Upset because of my stupidity. I knew what type of trouble taking pictures of him would get me into but I did it anyway. Because he was my obsession. Why couldn't I just tell him that?

He turned his back on me and headed out of the bedroom. I crawled to the edge of the bed, until there was no more left. Standing to my feet, I slowly followed behind him, calling his name. But he didn't say anything. Stepping on pieces of my camera, I was reminded of what I was without. Everything I've done. The memories. The breathtaking sunrises, and sunsets. The busy hustle and bustle of down town Detroit. The monuments. Snapshots of him. My favorite muse. Photos I wanted to cherish forever, now lied in his basketball shorts on a fragile memory card. In a matter of seconds, it could all be gone.

"Cass—

"Get out before I do some shit I'll regret," he coldly told me before slamming the door to the bathroom in my face.

I flinched and wrapped my arms around my naked body.

"I just—

BOOM!

He punched a hole in the door, and I jumped back at the sight of his black fist.

"Fuck out of my crib, shorty," he yelled, sending vibrations through my body again.

I hurried my ass back to the room to grab my things. I had never gotten dressed so fast in my life. I was out of his house in less than three minutes.

*

I climbed into Omni's car, and turned away from her. I didn't want her to see me in my feelings like this. This shit was new for me. I never allowed myself to get open enough to allow someone to hurt me. But Cass... he had my heart. I had finally let my guard down and allowed myself to fall.

"You had sex with him, Ryann," asked Omni, in a voice heavily coated with judgment as she pulled away from the gate. "Damn, poor Dinero."

"*What*," I asked, whipping my head in her direction.

She ran her hand through her curly hair, "People just don't respect relationships anymore. I swear that's so fucking bold."

"Fuck Dinero, and fuck your judgment," I spat.

I didn't know what was wrong with Omni, and I really didn't give a fuck. She was most likely mad at Juice ass. But who she should be mad at is herself. Omni's little perfect vision of her relationship with my brother was obviously fading and she was finally beginning to see what the rest of the world had always saw—that Juice wasn't shit. So, she felt some type away about infidelity.

"I'm just saying...we've been trying to reach you all night, and you're over here fucking with Cass."

"Reach me for what," I yelled. "I am a grown ass woman I can come and go as I please. The fuck?"

She smashed down on the brakes and turned to face me.

"That man needed your ass last night," she yelled with tears in her eyes. "Peewee got shot last night, Ry!"

"What," I asked, as my heart dropped to the pit of my stomach. "Is he okay?"

"While you were cheating on him, he was rushing his little brother to the hospital with a bullet in his fuckin' back."

- Cass -

Ryann had just left my crib, and I was sitting in my office, at my computer, flipping through the photos on the memory card I scooped up.

"This shit is wild yo," I said out loud to myself as I sat at my desk, flicking through the pictures in amazement.

Couple minutes ago, things got crazy between Ryann and I. I almost killed her stupid ass.

I had been having one of those nights, and couldn't sleep. So, I was up early as shit. I saw her camera sitting on the nightstand, and picked it up. I wasn't trying to invade her privacy. Shit, she's a photographer and I wanted to see what kind of magic she'd been shooting. I didn't expect to see pictures of myself flooding that bitch. My thoughts immediately went on 'noid shit. Was she working with the FEDs? Broad jumped on the gun charge a lil' too easily, feel me? Them boys were probably blowing her cover so she had to say something to get herself out of a rut, right? Could be. Shit sounded about legit.

Sitting there, all kinds of thoughts swam through my mind. That day on the balcony crossed my mind. That day when I was shooting the shit with Chicago...All that. Those times, it had to be her. Broad had to be a FED. And when I came acorss those pictures of me from those days, I was given all of the confirmation I needed.

Damn, is this what it came down to? The moment I think I found me a solid one, she turn out to be a fraud. This is why I do 'em the way I do 'em. I tried to do something different with girl. I was trying to date her before I blessed her with this dick. Because I thought she deserved that kind of respect. I can admit it, a nigga was thrown by a pretty face, a nice smile, and a stupid fatty. Aside from the physical qualities, I was attracted to her mind. Thought she was dope, and different from the rest. She walked around the hood with a fuckin' camera around her neck for fucks sake. Guess it was all for work.

For so long, shorty was flexing like she was into a nigga, but fuck... she was probably always so shook because she knew that at any given moment her cover could be blown and I'd snap her fuckin neck. Because that is exactly what I would do if she turned out to be a fuckin' pig.

I wouldn't give two fucks about the consequences. Niggas can't have a case with no body. And her brothers? Fuck 'em. I'd leave them niggas just as lifeless as their beloved sister if it came down to it. Fuck...I'm talking about a body and just a minute ago, I couldn't even murk her.

I took a long pull from the blunt I was chiefing on, and then inhaled the thick cloud of smoke before it could fade off into the darkness of my office. It was the darkest room in the house, with the black drapes pulled, warranting out all sunlight. I wasn't in a sunlight type of mood. My mood was just as dark as the room I sat in. Ryann had no idea how close she was to meeting the same demise so many others had met.

I was pissed beyond reasoning, but I couldn't kill her. With her, I was rational. I wanted to cross every t and dot every i. She had a hold on me, and I hated that shit. Before Ryann, I didn't give a fuck. Before Ryann, I didn't have anybody. Nothing but the drugs, and the money, and a couple cats who only fucked with me because I laced them with bread and because they knew that if they crossed me they'd die. None of the shit in my life was genuine. Not until I met her. She was like that first home cooked meal after doing a ten year bid or some shit. Now, I didn't know what was what between us and it ate at me viciously.

Takin' a mafuckas life came easy for me. I didn't care about shit like that. I looked at it like I was doing what I was put here to do. Had that been Genie, or any other bird bitch, she'd be dead. Chicago and a couple other cats would be wrapping her body in plastic at this very moment. With Ryann I was careful. Without her I was a fuckin' maniac.

My phone rang and I quickly snatched it up from the desk.

"What you got for me, Scotty," I answered.

"Clean as a whistle. Well, except the gun charge she took for you."

"I know she's clean, G. I need to know if she's a FED."

Scotty chuckled, "A Mosley? A FED—

"I don't give a fuck about her last name. Don't you think I thought about all of that shit, Scotty? Stop beating around the fuckin' bush and tell me what it is I want to know," I snapped.

Scotty cleared his throat, "My apologies. No, she's no FED. She's a photographer. Nothing more, nothing less."

She was much more than just a photographer. She was special to me, and I snapped on her on some reckless shit.

I hung up on him, snatched the memory card out of the slot, and left the crib.

*

"Yo, Ryann in there," I asked the girl sitting on Ryann's porch.

She shook her head no, "Naw, she's down at the hospital."

I didn't know what it was, but there was something crazy familiar about shorty. She looked a lot like Ryann's cousin Ashlee, but that wasn't it. I couldn't put a finger on it, but I knew her from somewhere. She must've been kicking it with Ry the many times I pulled up on her. That had to be it.

"How are you, Cass," she asked with a smile as she crossed one leg over the other.

I scratched my cheek, "I'm smooth. Ay, what hospital she at? What for?"

"Sinai. Her *boyfriend's* brother got shot," she said adding extra emphasis on boyfriend like I didn't know Ryann had one of those. Everybody knew I was well aware of that shit and didn't give a damn.

I nodded, "Oh, aight."

I turned to leave and she yelled out, "You don't remember me?"

I looked over my shoulder at her, "Am I supposed to?"

She stood up, shook her head, and went into the house. I stood there a minute, confused as hell until Chicago jogged across the street.

"Shorty still nuts about you," he said with a laugh.

"Who the fuck is that," I asked as I headed to my whip.

I didn't know that bitch, and the fact that she knew Ryann didn't sit too well with me either. Especially since Chicago just said she was crazy about me. I didn't need anybody trying to fuck up what I was trying to build with baby. Hell, I've probably already messed that up myself. Shit.

"That runner," he said with a snort. "Remember nigga? She was at the trap a couple nights ago gettin a train ran on her by Wavy, Nino, and a couple other niggas. Bitch kept trying to get you to come in the room, but you wasn't havin it. She threw a whole ass tantrum, hopped off Wavy dick and stormed out of the trap half naked." He laughed, "Bitch a real ass nut job, G."

I cocked my head to the side a little, thinking. What he said started to come back to me, and I then figured out where I knew her from. Bitch was just as nutty as he said she was. She stayed waving, speaking, and all that before I saw her at the trap. She came through for weed, and finessed her way inside.

Whole time she was there, she kept trying to throw the pussy at me. I was in a fucked up mood because Ryann had been curving me. Girl was one of those type bitches that did anything for attention. I wasn't giving her what she wanted so I guess she felt like fuckin' a team of niggas would peak my interest.

Why? Shit boggles my mind. But that's what she did. Bird had the nerve to call me into the room like that gay shit enticed me. Fuck I look like sharing pussy in a room full of niggas? Whole time they were stickin' dick to her, she was moaning my name. Shit was legit weird as hell, and I spazzed on her.

"Who is she to Ryann," I asked. That's all I gave a fuck about.

Chicago sucked his teeth, "Cousin."

My eyes widened, "Straight?"

"Hell yeah."

I shook my head and grabbed the handle to my car door, "Aight nigga. I'll link with yall a lil' later. You got something for me?"

"Heard niggas had a lead on Maino and Rome. I'll hit you up when I hear more about it."

I nodded and hopped in the car, "Bet it up."

*

"What are you doing here," said Ryann pushed herself up from the chair she was sitting in.

I extended a Best Buy bag to her, "I owe you a new camera. Most importantly, I owe you an apology."

She looked me up and down and walked right by me, "You can keep both of them shits."

I dragged my top teeth over my bottom lip, and followed behind her, "I deserve that—

"Nah, nigga you deserve a lot more than that. But for the sake of this hospital being flooded with cops, I won't act a fool."

I grabbed her arm and she flinched away, "Listen, a nigga flipped on some paranoid shit. I mean, can you really blame me, sweetheart? Ya fuckin' camera was flooded with pictures of me. Shit's creepy as hell now that I think about it."

Her light skin turned red and she looked away. She looked down at the floor and then back up at me, "Art. It was fucking art."

She walked away again, and like a cornball, I followed right behind her. I didn't give a fuck about any of the people staring. I didn't give a fuck about her being at this bitch to support her dude or none of that. All I gave a fuck about was makin shit right with Ryann again. I can admit it, I was on some sucka shit. And that was because she had a nigga open. I've never been open over anybody. Hell, I didn't have a heart until she gave me hers.

"Ryann—

She quickly turned around and swiped a tear from her face, "What nigga? What in the fuck do you want? You on some disrespectful shit anyway. My boyfriend is literally upstairs, and will be down here at any given—

"Fuck outta here. You didn't give a fuck about me disrespecting with this dick last night. Nah, shorty. You were whimpering and shit, cummin' all over this mafucka. Now you want me to respect some shit, that you don't even respect? Where was the respect for ya dude then," I shot back with a smirk. "Ya feelings hurt, I get it. And I apologized—get out them mafuckas, sweetheart."

Ryann didn't say anything. She walked away, and I followed right behind her. I came at her raw but she was playing games I didn't want to play. Talm'bout respecting her relationship and all lat. When just last night she was talking about leaving the goofy. She was on straight fraud shit.

"You gone keep walking like you don't know I'm right here, my baby," I said as she stopped at the reception desk.

"Hi, is there any news on Patrick Brown's condition," she asked the lady averting her eyes between Ryann and I.

"Sweetie, are you okay? Do you need me to call security," she asked, concerned about the tears falling from Ryann's eyes.

"Yeah, she's good. Just in her feelings. You a woman, you should know a lot about that shit, huh," I asked leaning up against the desk. "I fucked around and hurt her feelings, and I'm trying to express to her how I'm sorry I am about that but she won't let me."

I was talking to the lady, but my eyes stayed on Ryann. I never meant to make her cry. Shit ate me up, and had me battling between grabbing her or just walking away. Grabbing her would mean she had me just as open as I'd tried to avoid. Walking away would hurt her more than I wanted to, but in a way it was necessary. But I couldn't fathom hurting her anymore.

So, I grabbed her arm and as expected, she tried to protest. Even punched me in the chest. I grabbed her wrist and pulled her into my arms, "Chill, baby. You see all these mafuckas watching? She ready to call security and shit. Is that what you want?"

"You wouldn't begin to imagine what it is that I want, Cassim," she yelled, yanking away from me. She wiped her face and turned to face the lady again, "Update on Patrick Brown, please?"

The receptionist sighed, and tapped around on her keyboard. She told Ryann that Peewee would be coming out of surgery shortly and would be in recovery for the next hour or so. Ryann nodded and walked away. I slipped my hand into hers, interlocking my fingers with hers. She tried to pull away again, but I just held onto her hand tighter.

"He's going to be looking for me," she said through tight lips.

"What's that gotta do with me," I asked. "Let me talk to you for a minute, sweetheart."

Ryann stopped trying to pull away, and gave in.

*

I snatched her phone from her hands and stuffed it into my pocket, "I thought we talked about that phone shit, love."

She sighed and crossed her arms over her chest, "What do you want, Cass?"

I licked my lips, and reached over to rub her cheek. As expected, she closed her eyes and a low sigh fell from her lips. No matter how mad Ryann got with me, she always succumbed to a nigga's touch.

"I didn't mean to make you cry—

She sucked her teeth, "Nigga I was crying about Peewee."

"C'mon my baby," I said calling her bullshit. "It is what it is. I hurt you and I didn't mean to. Aight? Shit, I thought you were a FED."

She jerked away from my touch and looked out of the window, "A fuckin' FED Cassim? Be real. The fuck I look like being a damn FED."

I shrugged and rubbed the stubble on my chin, "I mean, the collection of pictures... you creepin in the bushes... shit sounds a lil' FED'y to me, sweetheart."

Ryann sat on her hands and pulled her bottom lip in her mouth, "I get it."

"Look at me," I said, and as expected she turned my way. "I need honesty, Ryann. Can you give me that?"

She blinked and rolled her eyes up, "You must... you must think I'm crazy or something don't you?"

I shrugged, "Shit shorty. I don't know what to think, to be completely honest. If you want me to go off of the obnoxious number of pictures I found of me in your camera, then... yeaaaah I'd think you were a little crazy," I paused and grabbed her hands from underneath her thighs. "But, if you talk to me. Tell me why...what that shit was about... you know, get me to see it in another light...I'm sure that'll change what I'm thinking right now."

"I...I love all things beautiful, Cassim," she said, stammering over her words.

"Baby, relax," I told her as I gave her hand a light squeeze.

On most days, Ryann was a nervous wreck around me. Earlier, I thought I found out why. I thought it was because she was a FED. A rookie maybe? But nah, now that I know that's not even the case, I'm back at square one, wondering what the fuck she's always so nervous about.

She took a deep breath and blinked a few times before saying, "I'm a photographer. It is my passion, Cassim. I never...I never meant for things to get the way they got. Photographing you became a fuckin' addiction. I was obsessed with the beauty of you—

"C'mon now—

"Stop it Cass," she yelled. "You want honesty? Let me give it to you, aight?" She sighed again, "It all started out so innocent. Accidental, actually. It was the winter, and we had just gotten our first big snow. I was out in the garden doing what it is I do, capturing beauty. When you... you with your dark skin and thick locs... you stood in the way. What I thought was beautiful...what I thought deserved to be added to my collection of photos... was nothing in comparison to you. Standing there with the poise of a God... one of an African king... you demanded attention and that is what I gave you. I gave you all of my attention, Cass."

I sat there speechless listening to the way she talked about me. The passion in her voice, the way she described me and shit...it was different. So different that I didn't know how to respond to it.

"I should have stopped. But I couldn't, Cass," she said with furrowed eyebrows and misty eyes, "I couldn't. You became more than just a photogenic face. You became my addiction. I woke up looking forward to taking pictures of you. I woke up wondering what it was that you would wear, and how you would wear your hair. Every day, I hoped that you would let go the way you did at home, when you let your dreads hang freely. But you didn't and—

"Shorty..."

I was trying to let go of the fact that she'd been to my crib. Trying to ignore the fact that she had been in my backyard, invading my privacy. Her mentioning it reminded me of just how close I was to putting a bullet in her head.

She spoke about obsessing over taking pictures of me and all that, but I can't front like I'm not bothered by it. I don't really give a fuck about the pictures from the hood. I gave a fuck about the ones she took of me in the privacy of my own home. It all bothered me, but that bothered me the most.

"I'm sorry, Cass," she said as a tear crept down her face. She quickly swiped it away and pulled her hand out of mine. "Listen...all that shit I just said...please don't repeat it. I will never take another picture of you again. Thanks for the new camera, but you can keep it. I'll just get another one. It won't be a Canon EOS but it'll get the job done. Hell you can even keep the memory card. Good night Cass."

She went to grab the door handle, and I hit the locks, "Don't go."

Ryann was different. She stayed in the hood, and was related to some of the most notorious niggas in the murder game, but she was different. She didn't blend in with the rest of the people in the hood. She stood out, like splash of bright red paint on a white wall. And because she was different, I wanted her more.

I scratched the back of my head, "I get it, aight? You take ya shit serious, baby. Look at me Ryann."

She shook her head and said in a low voice, "I can't."

She was ashamed, and I understood. I understood more than just her embarrassment now. I understood her nervousness. I understood why at times I had to remind her to breath. Infatuation. Infatu-mothafuckin-ation.

I grabbed her body, and pulled her onto my lap, forcing her to face me. But she kept her eyes closed, "Open your eyes, sweetheart."

I could feel her heart beating through her shirt. She was so nervous. I wanted her to know that she had no reason to be.

She finally opened her eyes, and sighed, "I look so fuckin' stupid right now."

"Cut it out. You look beautiful. All the time, especially when you bussin' a nut," I said, trying to lighten the mood.

Her hands went up to her face, "Stoppppp, freak."

I pulled her hands away from her face and kissed her on the lips, "Do you forgive a nigga, gorgeous?"

She wrapped her arms around my neck and kissed me again, "Yes, I forgive you Cassim." She paused and asked, "So... so what now?"

"Now we move on," I said slightly gripping her chin.

"I don't understand," she replied with furrowed eyebrows. "You know I was on some creep shit, and you still want to...want to fuck with me?" She began to just rambling on and on, and I didn't give a fuck about any of it anymore.

"Calm down. I get it. I respect the art. Peep though, from now on, if you want to take a picture of me, just ask."

"Seriously?"

"Seriously."

- Ryann -

I grabbed the Best Buy bag from his hand and was shocked.

"Ow," I said, shaking my hand a little.

"You know what they say about that spark?" Cass asked with a smirk.

I twisted my lips to the side, "Static electricity."

"Nah, sweetheart. It's deeper than that," he joked as he pointed at his head.

Cass found me. I didn't know how he found me, but he did, like he always did. Sometimes I thought the nigga had a tracking device on me because he was always around. He was around a lot more than he was before. His black ass couldn't get enough of me.

I climbed back over to the passenger seat and opened the Best Buy bag. I gasped at the sight of the six thousand dollar Nikon D5 DSLR I'd been drooling over since it was released.

"I can't...No Cass...I cannot accept this. Seven thousand dollars for a damn camera," I said shaking my head.

"Six thousand, five hundred and the price isn't important. What matters is that I replaced the one I disrespectfully broke."

I chewed on my bottom lip and asked, "Why couldn't you just get the one you broke?"

"The best only deserves the best, gorgeous."

I've never had a man be so good to me...ever. I often wondered why. Why did he feel the need to treat me so good when I hadn't been my absolute best towards him? I was still in my relationship for crying out loud. It didn't matter that I spent ninety percent of my free time with Cass. The fact still remained—I was someone else's girlfriend. Yet, Cass treated me like I deserved a seven thousand dollar camera and Givenchy slides.

He'd just found out I had been stalking him, yet he bought me a camera and pulled me out of a hospital, refusing to accept no for an answer. The very hospital Dinero sat in waiting on his brother to come out of surgery.

Peewee was accidentally shot in the back by Perry. They were old enough to know not to play with guns, but too young to know how to handle them. No one knew where they got the gun from since Perry was too devastated to talk and Peewee had pretty much been unconscious since the whole thing unfolded. It was sad, but I was happy Peewee was still breathing.

"Thank you so much, Cassim," I said as I dramatically hugged the camera. "I swear I cannot wait to go crazy with this bitch."

"No more creeping through the bushes and shit, right shorty?" joked Cass.

Although we pretty much got past him finding the pictures, I was still slightly nervous and embarrassed by it.

I was a nervous wreck when I saw him walk into the hospital. I was so damn scared and embarrassed that I actually cried. Do you know how crazy I probably look to him now? Fucking insane, yo. He said that I didn't look anything but beautiful, but I didn't believe it. I felt like he would look at me differently now. I didn't like the shit, but I would try my best to move forward from it.

I playfully punched him in the arm, "Stop talking about that shit, Cass."

He held his hands up, "Aight, aight. You know I gotta fuck with you though, Beth Gallagher."

My eyebrows snapped together, "Fuck is Beth—"

"Bitch from Fatal Attraction," said Cass before cracking up laughing. "Yo, you never seen that shit?"

I punched him again and laughed, "Keep talking shit..."

He licked his lips, "What you gone do about it?"

"Shut you up," I replied with half a smirk.

"How?" he asked as he inched in closer to my face.

I looked away and blushed, "By putting this pussy in yo mouth."

"Mmm, is that right?" he asked with lust dripping from his voice.

My phone rang interrupting our moment. I knew who it was without even looking at the screen. Cass knew too and pulled away, sitting back in his seat.

"I'm sorry... I told you he would be looking for me."

Cass said nothing, as he combed his beard with a frown on his face.

"Cass—"

"That situation you got going on with ya dude... end it. I've given you time. I've accepted the creep in you. Now it's time for you to give me something I want. All of you. I can't share you, Ry. I won't."

*

Cass left and I put my new camera up before heading back into the hospital. Dinero called me before I could get inside and this time I answered.

"Hey, here I come."

"Where you at?" he asked sounding just a torn up about the situation as he was when I came here this morning.

"I needed a little air, I'm walking in now."

I know, I know... last night I said I was going to break up with him despite everything, but I couldn't. Not yet. Not after his little brother was shot in the back. I still have intentions on leaving him, I just have to be careful.

We hung up when I walked into the hospital. He was standing right at the entrance with Shonny waiting on me. Dinero pulled me into a hug and I reluctantly hugged him back.

"What did they say?" I asked as we pulled away from the hug.

"That the surgery was a success," said Dinero before sighing.

"Will he be able to walk?"

"They don't know yet," said Shonny, looking down at her shoes. "Hey, have you talked to Adrien? I've been calling him."

I sure in the hell hope Shonny don't think Adri is the 'be there for you' type of nigga. All he did was fuck her. He didn't care about her. I hated that my brothers stayed playing with these female's feelings. I told Shonny I hadn't heard from him although I had just talked to him before Cass pulled up on me.

She sucked her teeth and then proceeded to call him again.

"So," I said with a sigh as I stared into Dinero's puffy red eyes. "What now?"

He shrugged, "My parents are about to come back up here. I need to hit the crib, wash my ass, and clear my mind. You won't be too busy today will you?"

I didn't want to stay with Dinero, but I wasn't as heartless as my brothers. I couldn't turn my back on him during his time of need, so I told him I wouldn't be busy at all. It was the least I could do since he couldn't reach me last night.

Omni was talking all of that shit about me cheating but she covered for me. She told him after my gig, I got drunk and passed out at her house and wouldn't wake up. He believed it especially since I showed up at the hospital looking like shit, compliments to Cass for making a bitch cry and go crazy.

"Aight boo-baby," said Dinero before pulling me into another hug. He kissed the top of my head before walking off to greet his parents who'd just walked up to the reception desk.

I nodded and turned to leave, but before I could, Shonny stopped me.

"Ay, Ryann, can I talk to you for a minute?"

I looked over my shoulder at her and nodded, "Yeah, girl, sure."

I sighed, hoping she did not want to have a conversation about Adrien's ass.

Shonny walked alongside me as we headed out of the hospital. She sighed and stuffed her hands in the pocket of her cute cardigan.

"You remember Dinero's ex-girlfriend Veronica?"

I nodded, "Yeah, the one he was crazy about before we got together."

She nodded, "Do you know what happened between them?"

"He told me she cheated, why?"

Shonny shook her head, "He lied. Ronnie broke up with him because he had become too clingy... He tried to kill himself and she got a damn restraining order against him. I'm telling you to say this—be careful with him, okay? He's not as strong as he seems."

*

We were drunk as fuck.

I was drinking because what Shonny said had been eating at me something serious. And I felt like there was no way out of this miserable ass relationship. She didn't even know about Dinero putting my gun to his head, unless one of my cousins told her... but to my knowledge, she didn't know. So for her to come up to me about what happened between Dinero and Ronnie was crazy.

He was drinking because he just found out his little brother would be without the use of his legs. His momma had just called with the news right before he pulled up at my house. He was a wreck and had been buying bottle, after bottle, after bottle.

I was about ready to tap out because I didn't want what happened before with me forgetting shit to happen again, but it was like Dinero did not want me to stop. He kept filling my cup up after I told his ass I was smooth on it.

We were at my house, just the two of us. It was one of those dreary rainy days where couples usually laid up, watching tv, caking all day. I didn't know where my cousins were, probably somewhere getting dicked.

"Come on boo-baby, drank up with a nigga," he said as he poured yet another cup of Hennessey.

I sat on the couch with my head resting against my fist, with lazy eyes, "Nah, babe, I'm straight. I've had enough."

Dinero sucked his teeth and handed the cup to me, "You can't drink with me, Ry? Daaaamn shorty...all I need is a lil' fuckin support right now."

I rolled my eyes and snatched the cup from him, spilling a little in the process, "This is my last fuckin cup D."

He smiled and crashed down on the couch next to me. He put the bottle to his lips, and took a few sips before saying, "Drunk head is the best. I want some sloppy toppy after this shit."

"Whatever," I said, waving him off feeling intoxication creeping up on me to the point where I was starting to see double.

I slammed the cup on the table, "I can't with this shit."

I couldn't take another sip. I felt like I was about to puke all over the place. My head began to pound and the 6lack playing from the sound bar was so loud that it was like my damn eardrums were rattling.

I wanted a bitch who was down to Earth
But she want the God damn skies
List of my problems
Got this one on my line that won't stop fucking callin'
It's crazy I made her that way
Every time I see her out, I see the hate in her face
Like why you do that
Tell her you love her when next week you just want your space
Why you do why you do that
Tell her you want her but next week you do your own thing
Why you do why you do that...

"Bring that ass over here, Ry," said Dinero, pulling me onto his lap. "Trying to keep the pussy from me."

I didn't want him touching me period. After being touched on and loved on by Cass, I realized just how much I had been playing myself. But I was drunk and I couldn't fight him off.

"Stop, D," I said as I wildly pushed him away.

He grabbed my wrist and slammed my arms down to my sides, "Why you being stingy with the pussy, Ryann? You been letting somebody else fuck?"

I rolled my eyes and lazily sucked my teeth, "Di...Dinero, I don't..." I sighed, "Let me goooo, you hurtin me nigga."

He didn't let me go though. He roughly pressed his lips against mine and I jerked my head away. He let go of my arms and forcefully grabbed the sides of my face, keeping my head straight. I tried to fight him off, but after a while, my arms gave out. And right after, I passed out.

*

I woke up the next day, in bed naked, confused, and with a killer hang over.

Turning over, I was face to face with Dinero. What did I do? I fucked him? A feeling of disgust came over me and I threw up, and all over him. You think I gave a fuck about him jumping up going off? Nope. I climbed out of the bed and headed down to the bathroom,with my mouth covered as more throw up spewed from it.

I fell to my knees and put my face in the toilet bowl, puking my guts out. How much did I drink last night? All I could remember was Dinero passing me drink, after drink, after drink. I couldn't remember anything past the last drink he gave me and I hated that shit. Especially since I had disrespected my pussy by letting him slide in. I wasn't supposed to have sex with him again. Not after fucking Cass. But I did. Being drunk always brought the freak out of me. But knowing that I was done with fucking him, I'm sure I would have put up some kind of fight.

The evidence of last night lied dry on my thigh and I felt sick once again. Cum. He came inside of me. I let him hit me raw? What the fuck was I thinking? Swear to God I'm not drinking again.

I reached up and flushed the toilet before standing to my feet. My head was spinning as I walked over to the sink to wash my mouth out. Looking in the mirror, I jumped back at the sight of hand prints on my neck. Did this come from Cass? Or last night with Dinero?

He came into the bathroom and pushed me aside as he stood at the sink washing my throw up off his face, "Damn, Ry."

"You fucked me raw last night, Dinero?" I asked as I punched him the back.

He sucked his teeth and flinched away, "Nah, shit...I don't know. We were drunk as hell."

I delicately wrapped my hands around my neck, "What happened to my neck?"

He smirked, "Shit got a little wild. I can remember that. You kept telling me to choke you."

I walked away from the sink and stood at the tub where I started the shower. Staring at the water cascade from the showerhead, I tried to recollect what happened last night.

I flinched when I felt Dinero wrap his arms around my naked body, "Can I climb in with you—"

"No, Dinero. You can shower after I finish. Close the door on your way out, please," I said as I climbed into the shower and pulled the shower curtain back.

Dinero stood there briefly before saying, "Aight, Ry. I'ma wash my ass down at my mom's crib, then go check on little bro. I'll call you later."

"K."

The bathroom door closed and I slid down the wall and sat in the tub while the shower water washed away the sins of last night.

- Cass -

Rome and Maino had been found. Dead, rotting. No way in fuck these dudes could have given my mans Mitch the Snitch that battery acid. They were dead well before he was.

I paced the dark alley, looking down at their deteriorating bodies with three niggas standing behind me – Luck, Chicago, and Wavy – waiting on me to speak. I had been pacing for about five, ten minutes, contemplating my next move.

On top of finding Rome and Maino, I had a name. The name of a rat. Scotty couldn't give me the name of the undercover FED who was on my case, of course, but the name he gave me was good enough. Still, I didn't know who Wendell Stinson was because I only called these niggas by their street names. We didn't exchange government names, the only nigga I knew by his birth name was Luck and it sure wasn't no weak ass Wendell. I had a good idea of just who the fuck Wendell was. Wavy. It had to be Wavy.

It was Wavy who delivered the news about Mitch getting the bad batch and this niggas name and nick name both started with W's.

"Yo, Wav... who told you these dead ass niggas gave Mitch battery acid," I asked with my eyes locked on his.

He ran his hand over the top of his head, "Shit nigga...you know how the hood talk. I heard the shit in passing."

"Straight? Nino told me you told him one of the crack head bitches told you that," said Chicago with his head cocked back in skepticism.

Wavy sucked his teeth, "That's a whole ass lie, my nigga."

I exchanged looks with Luck who was fumbling with the toothpick dangling from his mouth.

I jerked my head in a way that told Wavy to come here. I draped my arm over his shoulder and walked away from Chicago and Luck who stood at the end of the alley.

"Why'd you give Mitch the acid? He was about to rat on you wasn't he, pussy?"

Wavy's eyebrows snapped together, "What, G? I didn't give that nigga anything."

"Ayo! Wendell! I knew that was you my nigga," said the young cat I sent to name drop standing on the sidewalk, right outside of the alleyway.

There was only one person who responded to his name being called, and it wasn't Wavy.

It was Chicago.

*

"Charter me a jet. I need an alibi," I said to Luck as I gloved up.

He nodded and fished his phone from his pocket to do what I instructed, "Bet."

We were back at the same apartment building where I shot Keys through the back of the hand at. I was getting ready to commit another crime. This time though, I was ending a mafuckas life. I didn't give a shit about the crying, bitching, and moaning that Chicago was doing. His cries were falling on deaf ears. This nigga knew off top how I treated snitches. They didn't get stitches, they got tombstones—that is, if their families were lucky enough to find their bodies.

As soon as Chicago responded to his name being called, Luck and the young nigga I sent there to call 'em out, grabbed him, and tossed him in the back of the all-black van my young dawg pulled up in. Wavy was straight shook and had blown about ten blunts since the shit popped off. He just knew his life was about to be over. And it would have been if he would have responded to Wendell.

"I was in a bind, my nigga. A fuckin' bind. Them niggas was trying to place Gotti's murder on me. I couldn't do life in prison! I had to work with them. And then that nigga Mitch saw me hop out the FED car.... Man, I couldn't chance it."

Gotti use to work for me. I murked him about five months ago over skimming off the packs. This nigga dead ass been working for the FEDs since then? Thinking back on everything that happened since then had me shook. Ain't no telling what this bitch nigga been running his disloyal lips about.

I trusted this nigga with incriminating information. Chicago was my young dawg, the nigga I linked with every fuckin' morning. We use to shoot the shit heavy with fat blunts in heavy rotation, chopping it up about everything pertaining to this organization. Not once did I take this nigga for a snake. I would expect some ho shit like this from Wavy. Not a cat like Chicago.

"It's chartered, bruh," said Luck as I stood in front of Chicago searching his eyes for any hint of a real nigga.

What I saw before I found out he was Wendell Stinson... shit was gone. What sat in front of me a straight bitch.

"How long he say?" I asked, eager to rip this nigga Chicago's tongue out of his mouth.

"A lil' bit," replied Luck with his arms crossed over his chest.

I nodded and told Wavy to grab the sides of Chicago's face while I grabbed his tongue with the pliers. Wavy eagerly hopped up from the concrete floor of the apartment building and did as he was told. Chicago was tied to a chair, so his arms and feet weren't a problem. I needed the niggas head to stay in place while I ripped his shit out.

He yelled and screamed for help like he didn't know that there weren't any neighbors for miles. The building we was posted up at was in Highland Park, MI, in one of the most deteriorating neighborhoods in the city. Nobody stayed around these parts.

I stood in front of Chicago with the pliers in my hands and he tried to bite at me.

"Bite me and ya mom's will suffer," I threatened.

He swallowed and nodded, finally wanting to cooperate. Chicago's momma was his heart. I knew his whole family. These niggas in the game with whole ass families were easy targets. How easy it was for me to get at them, had me wondering if a nigga would ever be able to hold Ryann over my head like how I did them.

I grabbed Chicago's tongue with the pliers and cut it clean off with a pair of scissors I had in my other hand.

"Ahhhhhhh," he yelled.

Luck turned away from the scene and Wavy cracked up laughing.

"Shit, bruh," he said.

"Shut the fuck up, Wavy, and keep the nigga still," I snapped.

I wanted to have as much fun with him as I could before I had to dip. I was coming right back, but the point was that I needed to do as much damage as I could before I had to hop on the jet.

Fifteen minutes, a tongue, and a mouth full of teeth later, it was time to get my alibi in place.

I handed Caesar, the pilot, my ID before he checked it and I continued to the back of the private plane. Luck did the same thing and we headed to Atlantic City, where I would spend about two hours gambling and booking a room that Luck would stay in, posing as me while I stayed back in Michigan torturing Chicago for three days.

- **Ryann** -

Where was he?

It had been days since I last seen or heard from Cass. The last time I saw him, things were perfect between us. I mean, yeah, it was right after he found out about me taking pictures of him. But shit, he'd bought me a camera, kissed me, and all that. So everything was good. To my knowledge it was. Was he mad about me kicking it with Dinero all night? He knew I was trying to be there for him since he had damn near loss his brother. He knew I was trying to let him down easy too, so what was up? He hadn't replied to any of my text messages or anything.

The last text I got from him was one that said he was thinking of me, right before Dinero and I started to drink that night after he found out Peewee wouldn't walk again. That was approximately eighty-four hours ago.

Was he done with me? I didn't know. He couldn't have been. So why was he ignoring me? I was paranoid as hell. My mind had begun to wander and my anxiety shot through the roof. Could he be hurt? Did he get into some shit? I didn't know what was up and it was driving me crazy. I had even driven to his house, but the man at the gate wouldn't let me through or tell me if Cass was home.

Every morning since I hadn't spoken to him, I've gone to the field to see if he would be standing in his usual spot. But he hadn't been. And this morning as I slipped my black leggings on, I wondered if his absence was a sign from God. Was this his way of telling me to leave this nigga alone? Did he want me to focus on my relationship? Was he trying to tell me that Cass was the kind of danger I didn't need to associate myself with? That couldn't be it. With Cass, I was my happiest. With Cass, I felt complete. Being without him for this long was torture. My every thought was about him.

Glancing over at a sleeping Dinero, I wished he would just get the fuck on. I was ready to leave his ass, but he'd been crying and in his feelings ever since Peewee was shot.

Since Cass had been missing, I hadn't uttered more than four words to Dinero, but he stayed in my face anyway. I was in a serious funk. Such a funk that I hadn't combed my hair or eaten more than a sandwich or a bag of chips. It was Omni who had to force me to do that. She was the only one who knew what I was going through without him.

The other day, when we were together and I was thinking about Cass, she expressed to me how she was worried about me. She was out of the loop so I filled her in on everything. I told her how I wanted nothing more to do with Dinero and how I just wanted to be with Cass because it was he who made me my happiest. Unlike the day when she picked me up, she was supportive and told me to follow my heart. But when I told her how crazy Dinero had been acting, she told me to take it easy. I was tired of taking it easy and just wanted him the fuck away from me.

I was sick of wearing masks for the sake of his sanity. I was emotionally done with Dinero. I just wanted to be done-done with him.

Anyway, I pulled my top down over my head and grabbed my camera. I pulled the strap over my body. I hadn't taken a single picture in days, but I only grabbed it so that Dinero's bitch ass wouldn't ask me what I was up to.

"Where you going?" asked Dinero startling me.

"To take pictures," I dryly tossed over my shoulder as I slid my rose gold Adidas on.

He turned over on his stomach and said, "Bring me some food back, aight babe?"

"Mmhmm," I said before leaving the room.

I wish he wasn't here. I didn't want him anywhere near me, but last night he said he didn't want to be alone. So, I let him spend the night. I didn't even sleep with him. I slept on the damn couch. He questioned why and I told him I just found the couch more comfortable. He knew something was up. He knew he was losing me, but he didn't care. He gave in to whatever I said these days for the sake of me not breaking up with him. Thing is though, that was happening regardless.

"You got some condoms," asked Ashlee, sticking her head out of her room.

"Bitch who you got in my house," I yelled with an attitude.

She looked over her shoulder and crept out of the room, ass naked.

"Loc," she whispered. "That nigga fucks like a maniac."

Annoyed. I was fuckin' annoyed.

"Go ask Dinero," I dryly said as I headed for the front door.

I didn't care that I had basically sent my cousin in the room with my boyfriend and she was butt ass naked. I didn't care about anything but finding Cass. I didn't care about anything but hearing his voice... seeing his face... feeling his lips on mine. Nothing else mattered.

She reached into the room and then closed the door behind her. Ashlee pulled her robe closed and followed behind me, "Ry... you alright?"

"No," I honestly replied.

"What's wrong?" she asked.

I swallowed and faced her, "I can't find him."

She narrowed her eyes at me, "Whoooo?"

I shrugged and continued out of the door, "Nobody. I'll be back."

I walked out of the house and she called after me, but I didn't answer.

Where was the sun? For the past three days, it's been cloudy and dry. Dark and dull, just like I had been. Everything had been off and I just knew things wouldn't return back to normal until I was with him.

My tank swayed in the summer wind as I followed the trail to the field where I stalked Cass at. I mumbled to myself about how he'd better be where he was supposed to be. I needed him to be there. I couldn't go another day without seeing him. I couldn't go another hour. I didn't want to spend another second without him.

I waved at one of the little girls sitting on the porch staring at me and she posed for a picture. I lifted my camera off my chest and placed it up to my face. I zoomed in on her cute little chubby chocolate face and took a picture of her. She then posed again and I got a full body shot of her in her cute floral sundress and little white sandals. She waved goodbye as I continued on my journey.

Butterflies fluttered over my head and then I felt them evade the pit of my stomach. My hands grew clammy as I got closer and closer to the spot I'd watch him from. The spot I'd stalk him from rather. The spot where I would watch him standing across the street, talking to one of his niggas. He hadn't been in that spot in days. The black hummer that frequently posted up there hadn't pulled up either.

I swallowed and begged God to let him be there. But when I looked across the field, there was nothing. Nothing but stillness. I stood there as stiff as a statue, wondering what had happened? Where was he? I needed to know. I had to know.

"Where the fuck is he?" I said loud enough to scare the sparrow that had been standing a few feet, away.

"You on ya Beth Gallagher shit this morning, huh?"

I quickly turned around and standing there with a smirk on his face was Cass. Instead of greeting him with a hug, I punched him in the chest.

"Where were you?"

"Don't matter—I'm here now, sweetheart," said Cass as he grabbed my wrist and pulled me into his chest.

*

His calloused hands brushed against my cheek and I closed my eyes. A soft moan escaped my parted lips, when his fingers brushed against them. So good. So got damn good to my soul. I needed this. I needed him. Without him, I had reached the edge of insanity. The realization of my addiction didn't hit until I was forced to be without my drug. I never wanted to be without him again. He gave me satisfaction in the most simplest ways. A smile, a head nod, a quick wassup, the twinkle in his eyes. It made me weak in the knees.

I was an addict and he was my drug. He was my sweetest obsession, the reason for the air in my lungs. He was who my soul craved for. But I often questioned... When did attraction become addiction? Was it the moment he placed his pillow soft lips upon mine? Or perhaps the moment he had a voice... when he was more than just a beautiful picture?

"You aight?" he asked with raised bushy eyebrows.

A question raised at my heavy breathing and the tears slow trickling down my face. With puffy red eyes, I blinked more tears away and gave him a quick head nod.

He held the sides of my face, staring into my brown irises with his cold black ones, in search of truth. Would he be able to see it? The addiction lying within me? The weakness as a result of being without him? Will he be able to see it? Or could he hear my soul crying out for him? Looking away, I feared that maybe he would. He'd already seen me in my most vulnerable state. Crying. Open. Full of emotion. Emotion brought on by being without him.

I never wanted to be without him again.

Life wasn't right. The shutter of my camera hadn't sounded. The world was dull and simply black and white without him. While he was away, time seemed to drag. What was only three days, felt like three decades. Left was right and right was left. Up was down and down was up. When he returned, birds chirped, and the sun came out of hiding.

I had purpose. Life had purpose.

I grabbed hold of his hand, closed my eyes, and kissed his fingertips.

"Look at me, Ryann," he demanded in his deep, baritone voice.

I opened my eyes and swallowed a knot in my throat.

"You aight?" he questioned again.

This time, I shook my head no. And a look of satisfaction, brought on by the truth, flashed across his face. Just briefly. He then pulled me into his strong arms, where I melted. Where I felt the most secure. He made me feel safer than a full clip. Safer than my brothers and a gang of niggas stomping behind them. All I needed was him. All I'd ever need was him. I never wanted something or someone as badly as I wanted him. Cassim was my guilty pleasure. What I craved. When I was without him, my every thought was centered on him.

His hands trailed down my body, down over the hump in my back, and finally onto my ass. He grabbed just under my ass cheeks and lifted me off my feet. I wrapped my legs around his waist and nestled my head in his neck. He then slickly slid my pussy down his throbbing dick.

I gasped when his dick began to poke at my spot. He wrapped his strong arms around me, while slamming his dick inside of me. His heavy balls smacked against my ass as I cried out in ecstasy. It was so good. Too good.

I threw my head back and he attacked my neck, viciously sucking, trying his damnedest to give me a passion mark. Something he knew was forbidden. Something he knew would stand out against my light skin. He didn't care, and I didn't neither. Not at the time. Not while his dick was buried deep inside of me. I didn't care, but afterward I would. Guilt would eat at me like a parasite.

I tried to push his face away from my neck with my head, and he grabbed my neck, steady fucking me like wild man, backing up against the wall.

"Fuck you doin' girl? Every inch of you belongs to me. While you're with me, while you're with him. Anytime, all of the time," he barked, pressing my back against the wall.

He then placed his mouth where it was before and bit me. I moaned and my pussy gushed. Cassim grabbed my ass cheeks and opened them so far apart that I thought he would rip them in two as he fucked me harder.

"Tell me," he whispered in my ear as he stirred his dick inside of my creamy walls.

"I'm yours," I replied, feeding his ego.

"Every inch. All of you," he grunted as he gave me deep long strokes.

He didn't know how true it was. He had no idea. I would lie down and die for him if necessary. And he would do the same for me. Just as he was my addiction, I was his. He craved for me just as much as I craved for him. Neither of us would admit it, but it was an unspoken truth.

"Yes, Cassim. All of me. I'm yours. Mind, body, and soul," I blurted out.

The moment the words left my lips, I regretted it. He was caught off guard by my admittance. He paused momentarily and his fiery eyes met mine, accompanied by bushy scrunched together eyebrows. Wrinkles creased his sweat glistened forehead. I looked away and he told me to look at him.

I did. What choice did I have? Cassim made me do things against my will. It was like my mind, body, and soul truly did belong to him. Not in a negative way. Not in a possessive way. I willingly gave him all of me, despite the fact that I belonged to someone else. It was only a title. Merely a relationship, but I was in it. I agreed to commit to someone, knowing I was addicted to Cassim. Knowing that he owned every inch of me. I could not love someone else. Not while my heart belonged to Cassim. As bad as the *inconvenience* I called my boyfriend was in my life, I would not be able to give him what he wanted. Commitment. Openness. True, raw love.

Why not just leave him? Fear.

Fear of the unknown paralyzed me. It scared me to the point of anxiety.

I stayed with *my inconvenience* because of familiarity. To call Cassim my man...to make it real...I didn't know if my heart could take it.

He lived the fast life. *My inconvenience*...he didn't. Cassim was a dope boy. Heavy in the streets. Unpredictable, ruthless, cold, just on the brink of psychopathy. He lived the type of life that I feared. The type of life that only ended in two ways; prison or death. Both of which petrified me. And he knew that. I wouldn't want him to ever leave the house. I would want him to stop slanging dope. But to ask him that would be like him asking me to give up photography.

As fucked up as it sounds, selling drugs was his passion. What he did best. Well, according to him that was what he did best. Shit, according to me, he fucked like a porn star. To me, that is what he did best. His dick spoke to my soul. His dick was like... magic. The things it made my body do. The convulsions. The curling of my toes. The rolling of my eyes to the back of my head. The way I bit down on my bottom lip, sometimes drawing blood. The way I growled like an animal. The love that nearly suffocated me when he blessed me with his dick. Magic. It was fucking magic.

He grabbed me by the waist as he moved away from the wall and carried me to the living room, where he tossed me on the couch. I looked over my shoulder at him, watching him come my way. That crooked dick bouncing with every step. My mouth salivated. Wanting to feel it in my mouth. I wanted it to poke at my tonsils. I wanted to swallow his dick whole. I wanted it all over my face. I wanted it on my lips. I wanted to make love to his dick with my mouth. I wanted to swallow every ounce of his cum.

I bit on my bottom lip and turned around. He stood in front of me and my hands immediately wrapped around it. Inching it down my throat, a light moan fell from his lips, driving me insane. He made me so crazy. I grabbed his waist and brought him closer to me, inching his dick further and further down my relaxed throat.

He grabbed the back of my head and I looked up at him. That look on his face. Eyebrows knitted together. Lips pulled into his mouth. Eyes closed. The look of pleasure. The look of submission. He was mine. He belonged to me. He was under my control.

He didn't like to be controlled, and as usual, the moment was short lived.

He grabbed the sides of my face and forcefully pulled me away from his dick. He then kneeled and pulled me by my waist, to the very edge of the couch. Cassim grabbed my legs and bent them back over my head. I held them up, while he dove tongue first in between my legs.

"Ahhh," I yelled, loving it.

Cassim loved it as well. Possibly more than I did.

He moaned in my pussy as he slurped and feasted on me like it was his last meal. He was in control. The way he preferred everything in his life. But in the midst of satisfaction, was anger. He was angry at the way I made him feel, yet he couldn't get enough of me. He ate at my pussy mercilessly, trying to teach me a lesson. He wanted me to know that he was always in control. But his frustrations only told me one thing; that he was losing control. Losing control when it came to me and it drove him crazy. How could he not see that I was losing control too? Losing myself in loving him.

I grabbed a handful of his dreads and he held the back of my hand, forcing me to push his head deeper into my pussy. Shit like his hunger for me drove me crazy in ways I never though imaginable. My eyes rolled to the back of my head as he lapped over my clit with his tongue at lightning speed. He attacked my pearl tongue with little to no regard of the wave of emotions he was putting me though. He preferred me this way. Animalistic, roaring, speaking in tongues, falling deeper in love with him. He fed my addiction the same way he fed the addiction of the addicts he served dope to.

When he stopped, I kept my eyes closed, my bottom lip in between my teeth, and legs steady held up over my head. Awaiting. Wanting. Feigning.

And then he slid it into me. In this position, he had full access to every inch of my pussy. Just the way he liked it. Cassim loved to make eye contact while fucking me. He loved to see the look of pure pleasure on my face. I loved to see it in his eyes too. I loved to watch him while he did things to my pussy that no man ever had.

I gasped as he filled me up. He was so deep inside of me that it felt like he was fucking my guts. He was his deepest; where he was his most comfortable. Where he let go completely. Where he was the Cassim the rest of the world knew nothing about. Vulnerability was sexy as shit on him. Watching him try to take control of his emotions, watching him trying to control his urge to nut...it sent me over the edge. Turned me on in ways only the furrow in his thick brows could.

I opened my eyes and met the fire behind his. He stared directly in the center of my pupils. There lied unspoken words. Three words that had yet to fall off either of ours lips. But staring into his eyes as he stared back into mine, I knew it was there. Those three words weren't needed. I didn't need to hear *I love you* to know that this man adored me.

I wrapped my arms around his neck and he held my ankles as he gave me long, deep strokes full of passion.

"Tell me you'll never leave again," I whispered loud enough for him to hear me. Yet he didn't respond.

"Promise me, Cassim—

"Stop," he said with a grunt.

Cassim was a man of his word and never made promises he could not keep. His silence was further validation, I needed not to make this thing official. But would it even matter? He didn't own the title of my boyfriend, but he damn sure owned my heart. I'd be destroyed either way. With or without him, if he left me again. If next time was permanent, I would die myself.

I looked away as tears wet my eyes. I hated this. I hated how fuckin' scared and in love he made me feel at the same time. This isn't right. To love someone this much? Insanity. It was fucking insane.

"Look at me," he said as he gave me long, deep, passion filled strokes.

I blinked tears away and met his pleasurable gaze.

I bit my bottom lip as he hit every sensitive nerve in my pussy. Cassim looked down at his glistening dick in amazement. My juices heavily coated his dick as I felt another orgasm sending my body into convulsions. He quickened his pace as he was on the brink of an orgasm of his own.

Our loud moans and groans echoed throughout every square inch of the massive home.

Cassim put my legs together, in the air, as he pounded into me. Knowing he was near climax, I tried to wiggle free. He stared into my brown eyes, with irises full of passionate rage, with absolutely no intentions on pulling out. He held me captive. I couldn't wiggle free, but at this point...at the highest point of ecstasy, I didn't want to.

I let him cum inside of me. And I'd never let anyone do that to me.

*

"Where were you?" I asked as I lied there wrapped in his strong arms.

"Handlin' business," he said as he massaged my scalp.

"I missed you... You couldn't text...call... nothing?"

"Nah baby. I wanted to bad as fuck but—"

"But why couldn't you just take me with you. You was fuckin off with a bitch or something?"

He honestly told me, "I was torturing a nigga for three days."

"Wait... what?"

"You talkin out cha ass so I kept it a band with you."

"You still could have text or something."

He did not understand what I went through. He didn't know how petrified I was. Being without him affected me in ways I never wanted to be affected in again. I didn't like it. I hated it.

"I didn't have my phone. Besides, you was aight. I'm sure you were occupied with the nigga you were supposed to leave well before I disappeared," he coldly said.

"I'm trying to," I said as I rolled my eyes to the back of my head.

"If you were trying, you wouldn't have pulled away when I was sucking on your neck a minute ago, sweetheart."

Should I tell him? I hadn't told Cass anything about the way Dinero had been acting. He didn't know Dinero threatened to kill himself if I left him. His crazy ass would probably offer to kill the nigga himself. I didn't tell him that I was worried about what Shonny said. I didn't tell him that the fear I had of leaving him was no longer based on Cassim's lifestyle alone. I was dead ass worried about some homicide, suicide shit popping off.

"Give me a little—

"I'm not giving you anymore time. I told you... time was of essence and I wasn't about to sit back being a whole ass side nigga, baby," said Cass shutting me up.

I had to leave him. I didn't have any other choice but to.

*

A week had passed since Cass came back and he was still on me about leaving Dinero. Thing is, I'd been trying to. But things had been crazy down at the hospital with Peewee and he was barely ever around. I felt like I owed him more than to break up with him through text message. That might have been the best thing to do since he was always too irrational when it came to me trying to leave his crazy ass.

After not seeing and barely talking to him for a week, he pops up ironically while I'm sitting on the couch reading directions for a pregnancy test. My period was a few days late and I was hella noid. That bitch showed up like clockwork every month. My shit was so dead on that I even came on at the same time of day. So when she didn't show up, I was worried.

I quickly tossed the unopened box behind me, but I wasn't fast enough and he'd seen it. His eyebrows knitted together and he quickly snatched it from behind me.

"You pregnant?" he asked with worry written all over his face.

I snatched it from his hands, "I obviously don't know yet."

Dinero ran his hand over his wave covered head and said, "Go take it."

"How is Peewee? Are things looking up?" I asked, trying to avoid taking the test in front of him.

"Yeah, his vitals are returning to normal and he's been eating," he quickly replied before telling me to go take the test again.

I sighed and pushed myself up from the couch, heading down to the bathroom. He tried to walk inside with me, but I put my hand up, blocking him.

"Wait," I said before closing the door in his face.

I pulled my shorts down and sat on the toilet staring at the stick, scared to take it. I still didn't know what went on between Dinero and I when I was drunk. He said he wasn't sure if he used a condom or not, and by the dry cum sitting on my thigh that day, I was sure that he didn't. And I knew for a fact that Cass came inside of me because I let him.

I leaned forward and pissed on the stick, then sat it on the counter. My leg bounced with anticipation as I thought about just how much a positive test would change everything. I would have to tell Cass that I was pregnant and that I didn't know who the baby would belong to. I would have to break his heart. I wasn't supposed to have sex with Dinero anymore. My pussy belonged to Cass. I told him that. Now I would have to tell him that I'd given it to Dinero. But...I was drunk... he would understand that, right? Shit no he wouldn't. Cass was a ticking time bomb and he's already been waiting long enough for me to officially be his. He would most likely be tired of my shit and just be done with me.

Knock. Knock. Knock.

"Ay baby, let me come in," said Dinero from the other side of the door.

I didn't want him in here with me. I wanted to experience this alone. My anxiety was already to the roof. My foot tapped against the white tile of the bathroom floor as I nervously chewed on my freshly manicured nails, staring at the test sitting on the sink.

I looked down at my Michael Kors watch. It was time to check the results.

"Ryann—

"Hold on, okay?"

"What does it say? Am I a daddy or what? This shit is fucked up. I should be—

"Shut up," I yelled. I sighed, "Please… just let me do this alone."

He fell silent and I picked the pregnancy test up. Staring at the two pink lines, a knot immediately grew in my throat.

"Ryann… am I a daddy?"

I looked down at the positive pregnancy test, speechless.

I didn't know. Not knowing fucked me up. Not knowing petrified me.

Life had a fucked up sense of humor. And I didn't find anything about this shit to be funny.

"Ryann—

"Dinero… go home! I'll call you," I yelled with a trembling voice, trying to figure out what I was going to do about this positive pregnancy test.

He banged on the door, "What the fuck do you mean go home?"

My eyebrows snapped together, as I began to have a flashback about the last night I had sex with Dinero. The tone of his voice when he asked me what I meant just go home was familiar…. It was of the same tone he used when I tried to push him off of me that night, when I told him to get the fuck out of my house and go home.

But he didn't leave. He pinned me down and forced my panties down.

"Dinero…. Did you rape me?"

Silence.

"Did you hear what the fuck I just asked you, nigga?" I yelled as I jumped up from the toilet.

"I'm sorry," he said before I heard the front door open.

I quickly snatched the bathroom door open and ran out of the bathroom trying to beat him before he left but he was already gone. I pulled my shorts up and ran for the front door, but he was already speeding from in front of the house. Tears fell from my eyes as I closed the door and snatched my phone from the coffee table. I called Goose and he answered almost immediately.

"What's good, Ry baby?"

"Dinero raped me," I said through clenched teeth as I sealed Dinero's fate.

To be continued